Troubles in Utopia

Robert Chasse

For Evelyne

CONTENTS

PART ONE

A Time Is Pierced

Tom Long and Jim Slim enter the room. Both are in tophats, knickers and swallow tails, with blue shirts open at the collar. They are lost but do not show it, having wandered this way from a Guided Tour. The room is full of high drifting personalities without plumes but nevertheless with family names that have long histories.

Marcus Aurelius Prayer, Chief of Protocol, approaches Tom and Slim, his head pressed between his hands. He walks with a waddle, on the back of his heels. His nose is tumefied, his voice is full of qualms.

"Are you real?" is his first question.

Jim Slim — a full five seven — steps forward to knock the Chief of Protocol on the head. He knocks twice, saying, "Real enough, grouper."

Marcus Aurelius falls back two steps and gasps: "What violence is this? What manner of digaloons are you? Guards! Guards!"

"Digaloons?" Tom Long repeats. "What are digaloons?"

Marcus Aurelius shrieks: "A loon who digs— a digging baboon— a you-you—"

By now the guards and three-quarters of the room have assembled. Three men shake their fists, the others merely lick their chops. This is a fine beginning.

Tom leans forward and Slim whispers, "I think they're nuts."

"What is going on here?"

The assembly to a man turns to face the Person of the Secretary of Defense, Henry Howard Hungry, a mixture of blood and spit still on his lips, though he smiles broadly and seems magnanimous. He has a bullet-head surrounding his one eye (the other is glass) but his jacket closes properly and his fingernails are clean. There is a mark of respect which only the Great Men of the world know how to elicit, so the assembly has cleared a path between the Secretary and the two in their outlandish getup.

"Need I repeat my query?" The Secretary asks. His eye blinks.

"I see why they make em up when they go on television," Slim whispers.

And Tom whispers back, "What can I tell you?" And he steps forward. "Sir. We came on a guided tour—"

"Don't be insipid," the Secretary growls. A chorus rises around them, saying yeah yeah yeah.

"Well," says Tom, "which is the way out?"

"Unpatriotic scum!" — a voice shouts back — "the way out, is it?"

"Bring out the bloodhounds," somebody yells behind them, "the needlesuckers, the pitmouths."

Slim and Tom pass through French doors, bringing the glass with them, onto a colonnaded veranda (the kind seen in movies, where the adulterous lovers — there were no others — came out to talk, the ballroom music drifting from behind them; Ah nights on the swillbarge, reciting incantations at the moon), and leap into the garden.

It is called the Garden of Wonders, formerly the Garden of Sorrows, after the old tale that whispers of Washington bringing Martha here in order to kick her in the bloomers, got his foot caught in some local paraphernalia: it set the precedent for bringing in a team of doctors to operate on the Ultimate Executive's great toe. He never knew what hit him. He had to wear a yellow ribbon round his toe stuffed in his Great Boot. Hence his limp, his scowl, and his propensity for telling lies of state. Hence also the expression 'lying in state' to indicate the permanence of the condition. All things, big and small, are derived from your Fathers.

"Do you believe in bloodhounds?" Slim asks.

"Sure," says Tom.

"Too bad," says Slim. "That means I'm not deceived by what I hear."

Indeed, some local constable has let loose his perfumed dogs, in an excess of zeal no doubt, to please his masters.

The two fugitives rush through the ornamentals and stumble out onto a path which immediately bifurcates, one branch turning right into a darker wood, full of silence and admonitions posted on every tree.

The woods however are quiet. Birds and other noisome insects have been banished from these Executive Arbors, so that when Heads of State prowl here, the outer silence may match the inner. (The last time they came, these Heads of State, they were three, and they were held high on three poles by their entourage, solemnly passing, spreading awe right and left.)

Longlegged, they hurdle a stream in a single bound and land almost with their noses stuck on a sign pointing further still into the dark. It reads, The Margump of Freudenitch. They rush on. And, as suddenly as their fright had started, it stops, and they stop, as of one mind.

"Why are we running?" Tom asks.

Slim shrugs, himself puzzled.

"Ridiculous," says Tom. "If the damn things catch up to us, I'll turn them into turnips."

Slim nods gravely. And they resume their approach to the Margump at a more leisurely pace.

The Margump of Freudenitch is a duly certified scientist, full of research grants in the name of progress and truly applied knowledge. His task is to seek only, in certain prescribed directions for the greater glory of anything that promises to make the Proper Parties a sum and a half. Neat of body and attire, sloppy of mind, but sharp as a pin in the in-bin, he never rubs his hands like Doctor Savannah (and never has he been chased by Captain Marvel), nor pats his pate: he does not even drool. He is perfectly ordinary, in a white smock and glasses without rims. He sports his hair a little long, à la Einstein, with eyes that twinkle like pinwheels, an intellectual of sorts, an extinguished diadem; or, as Willie the Shake might have said, a Pox, a Wonderful Fellow.

"I have rats here," the Margump says, ushering Tom and Slim in with a small flourish of the hand and mouth. "Rats and mice and also dogs and geese; monkeys, an orangutan they managed to sneak in for me— I have the key. I massage their egos.

"And naturally, I have access to a couple of hospitals for the retarded, a federal penitentiary or so—

"Of course, some colleagues, in other parts of the country, more favorably disposed to the necessities of research into human diseases, their germination, propagation, immediate and long term effects," he grits his teeth and snickers, "these colleagues have had the opportunity to watch the disintegrative progress of a disease without having to terminate the experiment artificially — prior to term, as we say in the trade — by being required to show concern for the health and even the recovery of the subject. Whatever has happened to the spirit of objective inquiry? Shall I digress?"

"No," says Tom. "Just show us around."

"Well, what precisely would you gentlemen want to see?"

"The way out," Slim suggests.

The eyes of the Margump of Freudenitch narrow to a couple of slits. "The way out?" he repeats, as if meditating. Ah ha, he thinks, they have been sent to check out my Consciousness Rating or my Patriotic Stance and Verve. He smiles knowingly. "A strange request, isn't it? All exits lead back into the same world, gentlemen. Everybody knows that."

He permits himself a little laugh as a demonstration of his acumen. "Even my monkeys have learned that lesson. Observe their desiccated demeanor..."

"Do you like to kill, doctor?" asks Slim casually.

"Heaven forbid! Still, necessity often requires that a life be taken here and there, and as the need arises, so I feel pressed into service, and..."

"Do you eat your victims, doctor?" Tom asks.

"Eat? victims? What in the name of all that is..."

6

"You are unaware then of the progress which has been made recently in this direction by your learned colleagues, doctor?"

"Unaware? unaware?" The Margump quivers: an assault upon his scientific integrity cannot be tolerated. "I'll have you know, sir, that although I am isolated here, shut off to a large extent, a burp, as it were, in the Greater History of What Matters, isolated and shut off except when I go home at night to mow the lawn with the wife and kids — I love my kids, I regret often how little time I have to spread over them... — well, I am in touch. I correspond with colleagues. I read all synopses, precis, digests, the lord knows there is a bunch of them. I am not unaware. I have, tentatively — I will admit — partaken of a morsel, now and again, and have only begun to organize the experiment in a systematic fashion. System is everything, you know. It would certainly be a boon to humanity if a portion of the poor could be devoted to this task. The lord knows there are enough of them."

"Does your preference run to dogs, monkeys or children, doctor?"

"Children, naturally. Dog has the coarser taste, preferred by your lowly savage..."

Tom turns to Slim and mutters, "He's off the wall."

Slim nods gravely. "Do I punch him in the mouth now?"

Before the matter can be taken any further, the Margump falls to the floor and feigns the identity of a turnip. However there are limits to the role of a turnip which even eminent scientists cannot overcome.

After a few moments, he arises. "Now gentlemen," he says, brushing his smock with an immaculate hand, "let's be serious, enough ribaldry and sinister jokes at the expense of science and her devoted servants."

"We were hoping sir, for instructions on the — how shall I put it — on the manner in which we could find ourselves — as it were — on the outside of this place, looking in?"

The Margump's eyes narrow, he flushes and raises a hand with an accusatory index finger.

"You are nothing but massagoons, dirty, sniveling, little massagoons. And you expect to get out of me chemical secrets for the other side. The Other Side!

"Do you hear me?" He screams with fulsome lung, "livid massagoons, disguised like a couple of foreigners! Who do you think you're fooling? I'll have you crated and shipped to the dungheap!"

He hops up and down to mark his point, in rhythm to the baying hounds in the distance.

"Hoist him to the rafter," Tom says. "Set all his rats loose."

"Stop! Stop! in the name of duly certified scientific inquiry, I command you to stop!"

"Throw a rotten tomato at him, Slim. Deprive him of his smock, throw his rubbers out in the rain!"

"Oh my god, my god," the Margump wails.

It is in exchange for leaving his house intact that the Margump escorts them to what turns out to be a Great Iron Door. It is black and brooding, as all doors are at tunnel's end, waiting; a door — like a moment in time — is on this side and that — a separation but also a passage, which seems to be the point here.

"This is the only way," the Margump says and proceeds to open the Great One only enough for the two of them to pass in single file.

And then they are beyond.

False Starts and the Garden of Sir John Garterplucker, known as Longthumb

"Weecome to utopia— weecome to utopia— weecome to utopia—" whines a voice out of a loudspeaker buried somewhere about; below, nearly concealed in the underbrush, is a dust covered box with a sign above it saying, *Take Me.*

Tom puts his hand in and comes out with a news release.

"My voice," — the release reads — "fresh as you hear it now above you, is already turned to ashes on the other side of that great iron door. *Its* world is gone, so is its frolic and sham. You have passed into tomorrow, dream world for which we have planned these many years, the ultimate ecstasy: a world without recourse—"

Slim kicks the dusty box over and the voice saying weecome stops. It is a pleasant silence which follows so he smiles and asks, "What do you think?"

"Seems like we've gone through a time warp."

"A time warp?"

"And this is paradise."

"I can see that," Slim says. He points to the right at a small garden of plastic trees under a sky the color of aluminum foil. Plastic deer drink aluminum water from a plastic fountain; a plastic dog raises a leg to a plastic sarcophagus; all of it covered with a thin layer of dust. A plaque in imitation bronze is posted at the gate, bearing an illegible inscription.

The path before them has turned to sand, as have the trees that were. In the distance they see, as though they were travelers out of old stories, the spires, gray and vague, of a city. Between them and it there is nothing, like a burden on the land.

"Do you think they forgot to put people in here?" Slim asks.

"I can't even figure out how they think," Tom replies. "But one thing is sure, the way out isn't the way we came."

So they pass from this site, leaving behind without regret the Door that is no more and the Plastic Garden accumulating generations of stillness, and proceed toward a few false starts.

The first of these was when they reached the urban scene at nightfall, with the familiar drone of auto engines rising to greet them, and the familiar stench in the air that told them home is such a place as this. But they were wrong. They had come upon the Night of the Engines, a museum piece composed of pink skies at dusk, lavender and brown cars sweeping the avenues, no one at the wheels: it was an automobile holiday, where cars have the freedom to cajole the streets till dawn, without drivers disturbing the holy monotony of engines by leaning crassly from the windows and whistling at the broads, itself a memory of a former joviality.

The second false start was in a narrow street on the way out of town. A metallic prostitute leaped out and grabbed Tom in her metallic arms and they fell, she pinning him to the ground, her metallic voice beginning to quake: "copulate, copulate, copulate—"

"Get off me, you bitch," he cried. With that she rose and disappeared into the woodwork.

The third was an encounter with a businessman. This was extremely promising since it is well known such men are wise to the ways of the world, attentive to any stirring. His head was in a barrel and his legs dangled over the side; he was flipping out coins that fell and collected in a large pan around, while the man slowly disappeared into the barrel; then he said, in reply to, "What's on, my man?"

"I am pursuing the greater good."

"Well, excuse me," began Tom.

"If you give a penny, let it jingle around in your hand first."

"Thank you, but..."

"What is, I say what is," says he lifting his hands to the sky, "the heaven of the businessman? It is the place where all pockets are full of holes and he is an open mouth at the bottom of every pantleg. It follows from this that the heaven of the rich businessman is the place where everybody is turned upside down and he has a collection basket beneath each."

"I usually piss my pay away," says Tom. "I didn't know that. But can I ask you—"

"And what is, I say what is, the nirvana of the businessman? It is the place where no one is except the business. And money rains from the sky into collection baskets."

"Yes but..."

"A sucker is shorn every which way. By this truth ye shall know them."

Tom threw up his hands and Slim stepped in with a coin that he placed under the belt of the businessman, next to the skin. The man did an immediate double flip and came up standing on his keg of coins.

"Oh that feels *so* good," he said, rolling his eyes back and shivering.

"Listen," Slim says, "we want the way out."

"Ahhhh!" said the businessman, breaking open a smile and spreading it around. "I have just the article, just the thing. I manufacture desires, by the way, if ever you're in need. But I'm always glad to run into a copy of the original.

"I won't say it but you two are lucky to have bumped into me."

With this he jumped down and went to a trunk from which he returned holding a bottle. The label said, Way Out.

"I have sunk a few dry wells in my day — who hasn't? live and learn? — but this is pure gold." He held up the bottle. "Here, gentlemen, it is. It promises to make the world whole again. The final product, the Ultimate Delight, the ambrosia of the mind, a mixture of every known intoxicant, with a secret assortment of spices and, and — oh subtlety — a thorazine chaser."

The other two looked skeptical, so the businessman scowled. "Aye?" said he with an Irish brogue, "you have some kind of moral objection to pleasure?"

Tom sensed the high tirade coming like a wind of sulfur dioxide so he kicked the man's pan, sending coins flying. Thus it came to pass that the man fell to his knees, weeping and calling to his coins, and running his fingers after them through the dirt. And Tom and Slim turned from him and toward the distant places, moving apace with their determination to be gone; and, once, they turned at the crest of a new-mown hill (and three men playing golf there) and saw the man on all fours round his barrel, howling, and then they passed to the downslope and saw him no more forever.

"I could eat a bear," Slim says.

And Tom nods, shielding his eyes, intent on the figure on a dark horse, beyond hailing distance, cape flying, bone head glowing in the sun.

"Look," Tom says, "I'm more philosophical than you..."

"That's because you didn't have as much Fizz Ed in high school," Slim says.

"True." And Tom is also about the same size as Slim, some five seven, though his head is larger and he has a longer nose and all white teeth. So they walk along in silence until Tom remembers he does not know where they are. He says:

"Make me a utopia, said Mrs. God to God one day, and he waved his hand and said, poof, you're a utopia. From this initial confusion sprang many others."

Slim meanwhile has spotted a walnut tree with last year's walnuts waiting on the ground. They sit down to eat walnuts and bananas off the banana tree. A squirrel comes by and waves at them. Clouds drift as clouds will. And below, on the valley floor, rises the ergot dream of New York City. But neither man is fool enough to abandon lunch for what both take privately to be a mirage. So they eat their bananas and walnuts and elbow one another now and then over some common memory. Finally, replenished and groggy, they sweep aside walnut shells and banana peels to make room for their bodies to settle into, that they may thus gather slumber unto themselves and be rejuvenated. The thought has come to both of them that the journey may be long and the fields mined.

A voice awakens them with a British accent, "My word!" And Slim, before another sound can pass, has pounced on the man and applied the deadly Barbarian Eviscerator. That is, the man's ears are between Slim's fingers and the man's nose is altogether inside Slim's mouth. The next step is to yank out the ears, bite off the nose and watch the offender's brains leak out the three portals; hence the title of the hold, Barbarian Eviscerator, a hold which goes back to Timur Lame and is indeed credited to him. But, so the tale goes, pity on the wiseman to whom he had applied it had prompted Timur to stopper the flow half-way with an old cork and a pair of donkey ears. This image of the wiseman with a brown nose and donkey ears was rediscovered centuries later by Francisco Goya, and it is to this last rather than to Timur that our present doctors harken when, as of yore, they wag their ears reprovingly at us.

But Slim let go the hold and stepped back and watched the paunchy fellow dab his nose with a lace hanky.

"Ha ha ha," says he, on that tone. "I can see you fellows are urbanites. I recognized at once the fit of prehensile violence.

"Permit me to introduce myself. I am John Longthumb, Curator of the Magnificent Specimen you see gathered in the Valley below. It is the Museum of the City of New York."

By this time, the trio have advanced far enough toward the valley floor for Tom and Slim to see a turnstile and a white picket fence guarding his possession, the main gate topped by massive wooden ornaments, with the head of Joan of Arc impaled in duplicate.

The Curator huffs along behind them, quietly cursing his tumorous destiny. "It was such a marvelous place," he pants. "A true delight of incongruity, a masterful excrescence of stone and masonry, steel and bent dreams. What Curator would not be pleased as punch to lord over it now? (These cretins set a killing pace, he says to himself.) Hold up! Hold up! I say. My word!"

Tom and Slim pause before the stone mountains of the Grey One, awed by its towers absorbing light, even the air about has turned a murkish hue. Even here, in mausoleum form, it makes a man quiver to behold it. What brains had run amuck creating it? what dastardly desires razed it? what perfidy sucked upon it? The ancient expectation of its sinking beneath the sea never came to pass; and thus once again as so often before reality outflanked the Prophet. It ended in the pocket of a museum keeper.

They settle down on their haunches, and the other is grateful for their immobility. "What you see here," says Sir John, "is the physical monument. But I, I am in the possession of the veritable syntagma of the social and political history of that metropolis. May I suggest a small but significant illustration?"

"Why not?" Tom replies, wondering if this is another banana dream.

"It had in all its thousands of miles of boulevards and sidewalks only one foul street. I refer here to the men with dust pans and whisk brooms who went up and down Fifth Avenue all day collecting specks. The remainder of the city was immaculate to the point that they only sent in a large machine a couple of times a week — and in some places never — to drive down the middle of the street, calling forth the dust."

"I wonder," says Tom, "if you could point us in the general direction of the first town?"

Sir John laughs behind his cuff links. "I see you heard the story of the judge upon whom it devolved to decide — as a joke, mind you, a joke — to decide that dogs could defecate anyplace their brains told them to? Sir, it was a city devoid of dog feces. They wouldn't dream of letting dogs loose in sandboxes or public beaches. Such vile rumors have been expurgated from my texts."

Both Tom and Slim get to their feet. Sir John does not recognize the menace in that gesture.

"It was dirty," says Tom.

"Ha ha ha," laughs Sir John, full merrily in his manner. "That was one of their finest hours of urban planning. They systematically sprayed pollutants on the buildings, in the dead of night, knowing full well that a revelation of the true nature of this urban paradise would bring rustling to them a surfeit of the invidious, the crass and the miscreant. A genial act, on their part, these masterful, indeed even crafty, politicians: to appear gross, corrupt, even incompetent, to pollute the buildings by night and by day pass ordinances that implied the adjoining waters were open cesspools. Clever? Harken, gentlemen: they even colluded with newspapers to bring some noble ship captain to say in public — my word, I can quote this famous passage from memory — within 12 to 15 miles of the city shore, the captain said, there's nothing: it's a dead sea, the water is pea green for 14 miles out, then it's yellow from sulfuric acid, then it's blue gray from sludge, and all along the way you see nothing living in it, no bottom life, no baitfish, only a dark green slime all over. Magnificent! What superb imaging! But true? Tsk, tsk.

"If I may say, my good sirs, that city had the most monumental makework program ever devised by *Bureaucratis bureaucratis*. They planned to give traffic tickets to idle cars. Amusing name, no? — traffic ticket — innocuous — and I might add — inauspicious, for so grandiose a conception. Unquestionably genial, I say, as a sign of utmost caring for the citizenry.

"Tickets ranged between 15 and 25 dollars a piece. For this they mustered and deployed thousands and thousands of persons all in quaint blue, named policemen. Each one of these received upward of 25,000 dollars a piece, not counting fringe benefits, constabularies — precincts they called them — with a commander in each one, collecting twice the average rate, plus his retinue of saluters, papershufflers and telephone ears, plus a special unit to collect, plus judges, courts, court buildings, cars, trucks—"

"It wasn't necessary?" Slim asks.

"Necessary? Ah my good fellow! A simple arithmetical demonstration will elucidate the matter. It cost the city

15,586 dollars for each 15 dollar ticket. Necessary? My good sir! And do you know? the rate of collection was on the order of 1 to 5,000. Clearly their interests did not lie in the tickets per se, rather it was in the act of giving (the most gracious part of which was receiving). Now you will tell me such monumental solicitude for keeping idle hands busy was the act of a dirty city? a foul city? No, no; have faith, I have the records, the archives—. In such a haven, who could complain? who was unhappy? The nails perhaps that popped occasionally from wonderfully unseasoned wood they used to cover the boardwalks along the magnificently clear and clean ocean (without so much as a wrapper, can, tar, oil, or bird), and on such nails did careless children trip and rip their little legs or drive a thousand splinters in their hands? Nay, I say. For thoughtful men stood watch all along the quay to catch the clumsy little rascals.

"Whence, may I inquire? do you derive your very nearly fantastic impression of the place?"

"Well," says Tom, "I was there, once—"

Sir John bursts into a fit of uncontrollable laughter not unmixed with bitterness as he grasps the innuendo behind the comment, the sheer sarcasm of it and, bending his head too far forward in an effort to choke his laughter, he tumbles forth and rolls a goodly fifty yards, coming to a halt upside down against the picket fence.

As Tom and Slim amble on down with the possible intention of helping him extricate himself, Sadness strikes. It comes out of nowhere, well worn in its thieving ways, swift and sudden; and they respond in typical Slimian fashion, with a series of hollers and punches and headbutts (Tom even contributes a couple of kicks to the shins) until it flees from them, headlong down the valley, hair streaming, with Tom and Slim in pursuit. They make a scene, the three of them. It, badly frightened, naked and panting under a full length cape, and they, in swallow tails and knickers, flailing their arms through the trails of its hot and sticky breath. Finally, in a desperate desire to lose them, it enters a bog. They walk to the top of a hill to survey the terrain.

"Let's sit down here," Tom says. As it is, even if they wanted to, they could not find their way back to Sir John, who, not unlike certain beetles, might never be able to right himself again. He — Tom — remembers the story about the poor wretch who got locked up in a room and turned into a smelly beetle; but that was before the second world war, when the tale was taken by some as a presage of things to come, and no one would believe it.

They consider this, that Sir John might perish there, propped upside down against a picket fence.

"I think we have the wrong attitude," Tom says.

"I've been told that before," Slim says.

"Me too. But look, instead of looking for the way out, why don't we just listen and learn, like good denizens, and maybe somebody without knowing it will show us the way, and then we'll make our move."

"Sounds great," Slim says. "Now what?"

"Well, why don't we take a nap? It's warm and cosy here."

"You know," Slim says, patting the grass and snuggling into a comfortable position, and thinking of what they might have to listen to, "there are a lot of baloney mouths in the world."

"I know," Tom says. "But I've been told only good things can come from suffering." On second thought he adds, "And me, like an imbecile, I believed them." He sits up suddenly, for he thought he heard Sadness again, creeping up out of the bog. But no, it's only a couple of sparrows foraging among the dry leaves.

"And reality usually comes out upside down when they speak, relative to how I view it."

"That's deep," Slim says. So he sits up and looks around, with an eye to the distant hills and a desire to know what they conceal.

"Let's go," he says. And Tom nods in agreement. So they rise and brush themselves and walk down the hill until they come to a road and they take that to where it will lead them.

Dream Levitation

Slim, who was of old yclept Montezuma (a real loser in this word yclept, first encountered in Milton the eyeless), Slim had a dream and in his dream he and Tom were walking down these endless roads and he thought he saw a man carrying a sign writ with sacred text, to wit: The King is Dead; while the man intoned, "A long Hurrah for the Queen!"

"Who is the Queen?" Slim asked, an honest query.

And the man eyed him narrowly, shifting the placard from left to right shoulder, retorting the while, "Who is the King?"

"I don't know," Slim answered.

"Oh god," the man said, slapping his forehead. "Forgotten already. Oh you of transient memory! How mayst a man forget his presidents? A couple of cops, some generals, a bunch of lawyers, very impressive, very impressive indeed. One even sold peanuts and another neckties and yet another signed papers that came across his desk! I mean, it shows the inherent Greatness, the Lofty Contumely, the Sheer Moxie. Certainly the greatest of those was Grover McKinley.

"And what do you propose which is better, if you're so smart?" asked he, scowling like a man of substance. "Or, to put the question another way, how can you improve the perfect?

"Trust me, trust me, little man and small. So we're not perfect, you might say? Can you suggest any way for us to get beyond this, the penultimate achievement? I'll answer that for you: no. And why? Because human frailty can't get better than this."

"Shall I throw this baby out with the bathwater?" Slim asked in confusion.

"I think," the other answered solemnly, "I think we should because while we were keeping our eye on the bathwater somebody came up and half ate the baby."

And then he walked away, resuming his loud lament — Long Live et cetera — to the late forgotten Queen.

Meanwhile, an old man who had hobbled up to Tom began to reminisce about the time Chicago burned; put out only by tsunamis it was, from the lake, after the earthquake, by which time the city was wholly inhabited by the common cockroach and *ratus ratus ratus*.

"And generations of waters flowed over it and it collected sealife in its pores, and everything and its creatures smelled sweet again above the waves and the place was forgotten for a thousand years and some; and the fish verily swam elsewhere, and the critics languished in their graves; and the clover collected bees and he said, good show, my man, I am full satisfied with these my labors— And thence to nap, perchance, methinks, to see a languid cow rise drenched in smog and leap the incredible leap over yon natural satellite, yclept of yore the moon."

"Shall I question the wisdom of my fathers?" Tom asked, looking around for a stick to silence the old man.

"Castrate you, my son," the old man said solemnly; for, by his time, this phrase had become a blessing, not to be confused with an earlier practice for sharpening the tonal quality of male voices, or dealing with political prisoners.

Picnic Speeches

They top a rise and there she lies, full of bread and booty, resplendent in the sun, leaning her shadow to the left— the City, half-crazed with obscure desires, suffused with the arrogance of a dying species, like a Golden Horde upon the plain, throbbing. When they get closer they see it's more like a small town of squat and whitewashed buildings, with a hotdog stand in the central square, the all surrounded by a giant parking lot where birds and bees expire: from here people used to take their cars and speed off to nowhere. When they returned it was likened unto the prodigal son's reappearance in a Shopping Mall or Suburb, to suck on straws and talk about the color of overalls.

To ease the way to communication the city elders commissioned the creation of a Park with an empty rotunda and broken benches, a few squat trees with leaves curled by heat and fumes, and long circular paths to forestall, if not arrest, too intense a desire to congregate — agglutination it is called here — among the populace. And so one sees clearly the hand of the landscape architect, who patterned his approaches not as might be expected on the Avenue to the Valley of the Dead but on the Royal Way, that led to Angor Wat, flanked by giant squatted Buddhas gazing serenely across the Empty Faces of a thousand Christs; not only thus to show the sweep of his education but also to confound the opposition and leave them quarreling amongst themselves over the depth of the symbolism he has summoned from the Collective Unconscious (a repository of miscellany); and, indeed, the architect in his cunning has also placed, also in plaster of paris, a collection of his dearest detractors, with all their index fingers in various stages of pointing at each other.

And all around in every way, lurking as it were behind every tree, he has had placed Representative Statues of all, the little and big, the rotund, the servile, the fortunate and the inopportune, doctors and lawyers; generals and surgeons; scientists and astrologers; philosophers and priests; psychologists, palmists, reporters, politicians; policemen and thieves; bureaucrats and businessmen. Here one will find the reactionaries and those who are to the right of the reactionaries. And then of course there are the monarchists, the earlyists and the latists; the redeemers and bagists, the turnpikists and the official language, known as Pickleeze (its statue is a giant cucumber, in quartz, painted a modest pink).

The Park is full of speeches from men and women on rented soapboxes. Pedestrians stroll among them, savoring one, spitting out another; making speeches among themselves (these however, not being on rented time, are strictly illegal and generally frowned upon). Toward the center a man juggles three monkeys and a lead balloon; on the right a group is raising a flag in preparation for a picnic; in the back six musicians play with broken instruments; and further still magistrates sit on poles; on the left mothers play leapfrog with their children; and everywhere reporters take notes to convey their vision of reality. Sound documentation must needs precede the propagation of social amnesia. In the far corner a bunch of leftists are working their way out of the woodwork, carrying signs.

Tom and Slim wander through, in dusty tophats and duck tails, with grass stains on their knickers.

Billy Pan Bangem stands on a soapbox, Star Preacher, author of *Sacred Goblins and the Worms of Your Mind*. At his feet is a brown box marked, Solid Coin Only. The preacher has both hands raised over his head, palms facing the crowd; he rolls his head and eyes, a little spittle collects at the corners of his mouth from showering platitudes.

"Ah," sayeth the Preacher, "be ye like the blade of grass— look on it: it puzzles not, it thinks not, it wants not, yet cows grow fat upon it."

In the aisles people roll about for a little while then jump up to take a bow; God sits in the balcony, eating popcorn. Everybody waits in desperation for the stars to fall. What is to be gained here?

The Lost Souls turn to the two bizarros, their antennae evidently attuned to alien vibrations, and they scowl, a dark and menacing thing full of the love of humanity and little dogs and dead infidels. These good folk know intuitively that the road to heaven is paved with evil intentions. Whatever happened to the highest expression of man's spirit that used to inhabit religion?

It has fled through knell and dell to this region where Cerberus, quadricephalic dog of fame, for near two thousand year has let no one penetrate. It wanders now, the spirit of our being, in the aimless air. Once more the destiny of man has become a donkey dropping.

There is a miasma here which no amount of punching and kicking can dissipate. It is best to retreat, slowly, backwards, tipping the tophat repeatedly, to the tune of I beg your pardon and excuse me and so sorry and heavens to betsy.

But there are other soapboxes and other voices, loud and near, and one-eyed dogs devouring bones. It is after all the Park of the Opposition, where the most pressing questions of the day are confronted with such answers as will best tide the time over.

"It started out inconspicuously as a newspaper headline—" says the woman on the next box, a buxom lass of eight and twenty with golden tresses descending to her knees; a Mother Nature type with empty cupboards and pendant breasts, and eyes so shiny clear and bright they look like plastic marbles. At any rate she said it all began with a headline, 'Graft is the Milk of Officialdom.' This changed to Graft is the Milk (it would go from that to Graft is Milk to Milk is Graft to Graft is All), but before we got to that someone thought that Graft is the Milk which led the environmentalists to think Graft rather than being of the essence was an additive and therefore they took the only step they ever heard of: they sued; before a Court of Law, that is a Judge (a lawyer with a gavel) who, as reputation has it, knows everything since all questions are ultimately brought to judges to resolve according to their Prejudices. Which is (it must be said) a superior Prejudice since it mirrors — as Justice Oliver Wendell Frankfurter said — the Prejudices of the times."

"That may be, that may be," says General Cinderblock, whipping a passage through his neighbors with a hickory switch, "but if he's such a smartass let him enforce this decision."

"The ultimate question," says Mother Nature, ignoring the heckler, "the ultimate question, my fellow citizens, is not whether we are right or wrong but whether our Prejudices are in the right places. That is the essence of the Law—"

A little further on someone is shouting with equal gusto—

"I can assume tomorrow we will be taking the first step in the last lap toward the final solution to the auto emission problem— we plan to eliminate the people! I mean by that to deprive cars of the right to come out of their museums and enter our homes and roam about freely. Well, some will say, are we thus to deprive cars of their rights without due process? And I answer a thundering of yeses. I say unto you verily mankind has seen the day when cars can crash into our bedrooms *unannounced.*"

In the afternoon he will be informed that many years ago the cars revolted and withdrew to their own cities.

They come from the west end of the Park, like a breath out of a loonybin, a dozen or more (a reporter on his pad makes note of a numerous horde), they come in black leather jackets, swinging sausages, candycane and crosses. Their jackets are decorated with an eye to equal representation— skull and crossbones, iron crosses, left and right pointing swastikas. They are the official opposition to the official opposition.

The soapboxes empty. The crowds scatter. The children are so happy they are almost delirious. Even the lousy dogs wag their tails. For some time now these demonstrations of near joy at the moment of dispersal have disturbed the City Fathers. What does it matter that the politicians are sane? It is their arrangement which is psychotic.

Tom and Slim, with the ignorance of strangers in a strange town, have stood and stared like a couple of wooden Indians, arms crossed over chests, tophats slanted forward, looking lean and mean.

The little man that faces them, the leader of the pack, is full curly headed, with little dark eyes and lipstick incarnadine and a cowboy kerchief round his neck; he sports a cane.

"We are the Bugmouths, the Bugmouths. When we show, you gotta go. This is our turf, you dig? I mean, dad, we *allow* all this here jive talk but we don't take nobody for an answer, you dig?"

And the others form a little circle about their chief and cudgel and go a round of ring around the rosy, until he with a cool hand calls a halt to their praises.

"Check this, dad," says he, "the Reign of Asininity, arbitrarily dated to begin with the reign of Phillip II, lasted a thousand years."

"It did?"

"You better believe it, dad. I got that from the teach in fifth grade, dad. Hey, teach, I said, no shit? Believe it, he said, that's why we gotta had all these revolutions. I ain't one of these here dumb turkeys, peddlin' loose shit."

"Dumb turkey, dumb turkey," the others intone, lolling their heads.

"And let me tell you somethin' else, dad, we gonna beat that record! That's what we got here, a spirit of beatin', dig? like: beat em to the groun' an' beat em to a pulp and trounce em? an' stomp on em— an' all that there stuff. That's the name of the tune now, daddies."

"How about flagellation and immolation?" asks Tom, sarcastic as hell under a cocked tophat.

"By the gore," whispers Slim in glee, "I think you want to provoke these bugmouths." And he raises his voice to the modulations of a religious incantation— "Lily livered, chicken pluckin', cockroach screwin', jerk a dozen, bugmouths—"

And with that the Bugmouths fall swooning to the ground, and twist and squirm and squeal, expressing thus their titillation to excess, "that's our theme song, daddy! that's our theme song!"

And straightaway they arise and proceed to make Tom and Slim Honorary Members of the Temporal Lords and offer them sausages and candycane. And so what if the sausages are ten years old and a little waxy from all the use they've seen? It's the gesture that counts. One of the bugmouths runs over and tears down the flag that went up earlier and they spread for themselves an indigestible picnic of sausages, hard boiled eggs, pumpernickel bread, beer, a lot of guffaws and clowning around until darkness returns. The civic denizens of the Park do not sneak back in later, armed with police dogs, machineguns and outraged virtue. They all go home to watch television and talk about religion and the price of tea in China.

In the morning — and a fine morning it is on the edge of nowhere — Tom and Slim take their leave of the rowdies who, by now, engorged with beer and eggs, crawl around and talk to the grass and nibble at it, farting the while; others scratch their backs against poles and burp. It seems all basic, even rudimentary and fine, even the rudiments of a master race. The two in tophats walk to the cafe on the Square for coffee and toast.

The cafe is of the European variety, with an elegant outdoor veranda on which stand glass tables and wicker chairs. In the winter it is closed in with glass to keep out the chill rains and howling goblins that come from the north. It is owned by a former pornographer who used to sell dirty pictures in front of the railroad station before it was torn down. In this he was retrograde. He named his cafe, Sodomy and Gonnor'a, in memory of the twin goddesses that dominated his youth. He is at present a portly gentleman with a cigar and a quick smile, solicitous to the whims of his patrons. The coffee is a delight; they take it black; the toasts are dry and brittle as they should be. The hot dog vendor is not out yet, the organ grinder's monkey dances a saraband. In sum, it is a rosy morning, intoxicated with sun, almost sweet, — to be sure — it is sweet with the odor of clover and alfalfa.

Across the square and above the rooftops, the two men at breakfast can see people move against the flank of the hill. Tom is reminded. of the fields in the medieval age of Breughel— with dancing in one corner and sleeping in another and screwing in the third; threshing here, milking there; gathering straw in bundles; the all bathed in a soft brown and yellow light; it was a world that had reached a pinnacle in the existence of the species.

"The Lord helps those who help me," says the voice of a courtly gentleman, with a discreet nod of the head, left hand flourishing a little (as a boy he had dreamed of being a nobleman with a cape and had perfected the hand flourish that spreads the cape away). If Plato ever had an inkling of the physical appearance of his Philosopher, this man is it: tall and lean, of tiny bourgeois lineage, with hair swept back and the eyes set wide and the mouth thin and wide and the nostrils flared and the teeth long and hard.

"Pull up a chair," Slim says.

"May I? —Garçon, un café," says he with an indiscreet snap of the fingers, without looking back, but taking a seat and cracking a smile. "You gentlemen are new to our town, are you not? I find myself irresistibly drawn to strangers, as though in them it were possible to confirm my identity."

"It needs confirming?" asks Slim, with an eye to the man called Garçon, approaching with more coffee.

"Alas—" says he, become pensive. "Matters do not stand so simply."

The usually laconic Slim says to Tom in a stage whisper from behind the back of his hand, admitting a weakness, "I always wanted to shut up some philosopher."

Tom, dubious of the wisdom of such a desire, concentrates on his toasts and coffee.

"I was puzzled by your greeting, Mr.—?" Slim begins his interrogatory, turning to the Philosopher.

"Reginald Persay Boomchatter. Puzzled?" The wheels in his eyes turn, then a light comes on in there, saying Eureka. "The Lord helps? et cetera? It is a purely formal greeting that does not bear examination. What Lord? one could ask; and what can one understand when one says, help? and what is this nebulous category, those? Whereas a reference to 'me' lands us squarely in the thicket of identity. Like I said, heed it not, even if it calls to you in a dream."

"Some people," says Slim with a sly grin, "have solved this problem of identity— they know where all the doors are and all the roads and all the ways out."

"You have met such people?" Reginald leans forward, enthralled.

"Sure. All the crotchheads."

"He means," says Tom, chasing his toast with coffee, "the psychologists and psychiatrists, the psychoanalysts and psychosurgeons, the psychogeologists and psycholinguists, the psychonumerologists and psychohistorians, the psychopaths, psychedelics and psychotherapists, more numerous than the shattered face of christianity."

"Like I said, crotchheads," Slim says, irked that the obvious needs clarification. "They talk all the time about finding identity. Back home we have legions of them running around looking for it. They look everywhere, up and down, in all the closets and under rocks. And when you come to them the first thing they want to tell you is, I'm looking for identity, high and low.

"So my friend here," he jerks a thumb at Tom, accompanied with a warm smile, "he was going to write a book about it. He was going to call it the Freudianization of Fornication, if that had a nicer ring than Copulatory Freudianism, but anyone would have been quite correct to point out, so what? Why not Reichian panegyrics? Psychadubdub? Glurb-a-Durb? or Nurck-a-Slerp? Besides, what if he got sucked into the question, why was Dr. Freud's cabinet full of stone reliquary?

"Right away he realized the title, any one of them, enters the dangerous waters of speculation about the scientists who get their knickers wet by attaching electrodes to the copulatory organelia of indigent subjects as these perform beyond a simple pane of glass the ageless maneuvers, threatening thereby to introduce copulatio in vivo as a new Spectator Sport which might threaten baseball. Put it up against pornography, you got a chance. Call it art, maybe. But baseball? foot, basket and hand ball? soccer ball, pinball and roller-ball, volley ball and bocce? Never. He thought to call it enzombification, but what the hell? For that reason he knew his idea was a disaster. Even a prophet needs an audience.

"Anyway, to get back to these people looking around for identity. There are some others who think the problem is one of language. If you know the right words the problem evaporates. Poosh. They find the real thing is to identify *with*. So they identify with walls and doors and lost relatives and little dogs, flagpoles, insects, who knows?"

Reginald, meanwhile, has sat back and assumed a dreadful frown.

"I would myself find divinity in a rock if somebody paid me," he says.

"That so?"

"I mean by that, the crotchheads, dreadful term, pardon me if I say so; I found navelgazers so much more — how shall I say? — apropos, delicate, reminiscent of the shattered womb, and other delicate images— (he sighs); still, do we not say, shrinks? with its memories of rite de passage, high purpose and cannibalism? But to return to your crotchheads, they have their jargon, which anybody can use to keep busy. Can you blame them? We all do seek a mask, a cane, a prop, do we not? Yet in the final analysis, they have to come to us for a *conception* of identity."

"To you?"

28

"To us," says Boomchatter with quiet dignity. He remembers the years spent over the nature of the peripheral and the essential: how one inheres the other, but then if the essential is in the peripheral, by definition the essential does not exist; and without the essential there can be no peripheral. And last year, yes, last year, the long and dreadful argument with the person who refused to believe that language came to man as a Gift in a beetlenut which passed into man's saliva.

Why not, he remembers he had said, why the gawd not? Do you not see that what is significant is not the correctness of a theory of origins, but those tenets which can be derived from it? which can thus serve to guide us? toward those perilous goals we know not of?

His long slim fingers move like spiders on the table. And he remembers the lines, if Being is was-will-be, then was will-be and will-be is, and everyone is happy. *Ich bin*, as the Germans say, I've been always, such as I was, and therefore shall be, time without turmoil and adumbrations. And so he speaks—

"The whole question of identity must be referred to a larger issue, viz., the matter of being and time. How may we approach the matter? Let us hypothesize. And let us say, time is a moment of being, and that is not the same as being is a moment of time; for if you take a moment of being it is, by virtue of that very statement, out of time, and being out of time is not possible; accordingly a moment of being is not possible. But if you take a moment of time, being itself can only be infused *into it*, as it were, among others, unless of course one reduces ad absurdum to the proposition that time has being, or to the even more sticky, time is being.

"The two untenable propositions so far envisaged are first, that time is a moment of being, and second, that being is a moment of time. Since both have been demonstrated to be naught, one must perforce conclude that all who are in being are in effect dead. And yet, here we are, discussing it. That my friends, is the ultimate paradox, the dilemma that haunts the minds of thinking men." All this Persay Boomchatter delivered in a somber voice. Now a small storm cloud, six or seven inches in diameter, gathers over his head and begins to rain on him.

"Interesting," says Tom, returning empty cup to saucer.

Boomchatter, in a gesture of modesty, hides his face with both hands. "Well, I haven't been the Official Philosopher for over 30 years for nothing.

"Truth, remember, is my wherewithal. It has been my role, my métier, my lightstick, as the Germans put it. And the greatest truth is this, talk all you want but leave well enough alone."

With that he pops to his feet, turns to his lapel and says, "Okay, move in." It would be a mistake to think Reggie came suddenly to this pass.

Accordingly, the police rush the place. They come through every window and door, every crevice, every pore of the building, displaying a formidable arsenal of blackjacks and machineguns, crowbars and machinepistols, brace and bit and thumbscrews, and light howitzers. Some assume the famous crouch position, others kneel to put their hands on the floor so that when Fred Nailem Atacross enters he may walk on their fingers.

And in he comes, brushing little bugs off of his lapels, with a suspicious eye cocked, and to himself mumbling deprecating remarks about others (hasn't he seen the world? doesn't he know its vices? are not vices the core?); Master of the Situation, bearing only faint traces of a bout with distemper at the age of 33, principally a dolorous twitch of the right cheek and eyelid.

"Gentlemen," Reginald says, triumphant, "may I present the Police Commissioner." And turning to the Commish with a flourish, "You can smell the freedom of their spirit," he says, "it's disgusting. They need a stint in Penance House." From this position he falls to all fours to kiss the iron boot of Atacross which comes up to meet him and sends him rolling off until he comes to rest under a distant table.

"*I* am the Police," Atacross says.

This word — police — has an interesting etymology. Some authorities suggest it goes back through policy to polis (city), and that its first modern use comes by way of Fenelon's *Education of Girls*; but these roots are absurd on their faces: though police are large, no one has seen one as big as a city, and it is unlikely that anyone would entrust them with the education of girls. Historical sources here confirm that in the 18th century, lice from the Po Valley in Italy, began to multiply, as various species of the animal world have been known to do from time to time (one recalls the suicidal lemmings, trying to get off the Isle of Man, the locusts of the Middle East, the soldier ants of Africa, the rat migrations across the Russian steppe). In any event, these Po lice spread north then east and west, crossing the Alps into France and on into the low countries and Germany, crossing the Channel — or the Sleeve, as the French say — and the Atlantic to Britain and the Americas; the other way, they invaded the Balkans, spreading north to the Polish Sea, and east to the Carpathans and thence to Russia, the Middle East by way of Turkey, thence to Asia. It was the best the West could offer in memory of Sabutai or Subatei, the Golden Horde, even Attila whose hand may have been kissed by popes.

By the 19th century the Po lice were firmly entrenched, forming secret parts that would later give rise to a host of little ones, that would collectively acquire the name of the Seven Plagues. Its ubiquity led users to drop the capital P and bring the two words together to form a new common noun, police.

Still, the confusion about this matter has led others to suggest that the origin of the word is evident in Pol-ice, a reference to Polish ice imported by a now forgotten mayor for lining the pockets of his steamship cronies, this toward the end of the 19th century. A parallel source suggests it was the Chief who spoke no too good English who said, "by goolie, there go my stiff men, proud and stiff like pole ice (i.e., Polish ice)." These latter etymologies are however of doubtful authenticity.

As this was going on, Atacross, his nose reconstituted to make it hard, a realist, preparing to crossexamine the culpable, circled the table thrice, and crossed himself thrice and ate three lumps of sugar.

A fatal error, that.

The smell of sugar wafted upward through the nostrils of a sugar freak brings on an irresistible, irrepressible compulsion, similar to the insidious urge that brings cockroaches to grease. The police, even the ones with broken fingers, rushed the table and their chief, tearing at him and each other and the table. The feeding frenzy would last until all were consumed, leaving only, here and there, blue stains and an occasional whisker.

Tom and Slim were escorted out the back door by the ex-pornographer in short sleeves. He could not himself squeeze through the opening, and he sighed at the condition of his imprisonment, gesturing goodbye to them with little wiggles of his fingers.

They turned one last time to bid him farewell; it was then they saw, betwixt the legs of the chubby innkeeper, Reggie, still under the table, peering upward into his crotch, saying, "I perceive, gentlemen, the center of the universe—"

And so they went also from this town, called Dram of Plenty, in the time of the Sugar Frenzy. Tom and Slim, cool and clear and clean, sauntered and sometimes paced in the back alleys, past the pimps and warthogs, listening to the song of the moneychangers, the voices of old hags teaching little boys and girls their manners; the sight of men whipping their cars; and young boys and girls, hanging from windows and doorways, calling softly to their libido.

The Hills of Dram

They had not gone far, a half a league at best (that is about a mile and a half) when a guard pounced from the shoulder of the road, from behind a boulder there that could conceal six men, and interpolated them thus—

"Who goes there? You are trespassing in the No-no. You are under scrutiny. Precede the bayonet."

What he meant was that the General collects reporters, that Tom and Slim have been taken for reporters, and that they should now follow him, the guard.

He led them past the rock and culvert and into a line of trees. They saw, in a clearing there, three midgets playing craps, and a couple of crows watching them. He led them up the side of a hill where days before the grass had leaned against the wind and leans there still though it is gone. Their way is slowed by a company of ducks before them on the path to the crest. Once, in another age, armed men in black hats and prayers had escorted three hundred prisoners here and shot them. Does the Earth remember? Probably not.

On the darkling plain where now the host assembles, the ghosts of dead buffalo rush to and fro, and men armed with Winchesters slay them repeatedly. And Indians intone their death chants, beside their ponies; and there, it can be seen they die in bunches, or there, they walk into captivity. One end repeats the other. We tend to think history is what we remember or forget about it.

The guard stops a hundred paces from the motionless pennants and flags that flank the General's tent: flags in technicolor, pennants in black and white, and poles festooned with the death masks of his enemies.

The General, before the tent, wrists locked over buttocks, paces up and down, behind a long table draped in white and covered with maps. A small calling card on the corner says, General Edward Hail Drepanon, called Ironcoffin. On his right, at the far end of the table, sits his demiurge. And next to him is John Rake Demogorgon, mandrake hurler, policy advisor to the General, a runt of a man who just stepped out of a closet, smelling of mothballs.

He chooses this moment to hurl a mandrake root at the two intruders who have come within a foot of the table. When they do not flinch, he says, "they are not bewitched."

"The hell you say," breaks in the demiurge, scarlet. Then he reads a prepared statement: "I suggest they are an unnatural filament on our lenses and I propose we fit them each with a stick of dynamite between the teeth to see if their dentures will hold. Failure of this test will naturally prove them alien and bewitched and their passage shall be deemed no great loss."

He uses his index finger to penetrate the oral orifice and tidy up in there.

The General laughs with teeth bared, peering down at them, stiff as a ramrod. He sports a small mustache, no wider than the width of his nostrils, and a goatee, filed to a point; his mouth is tight, pinched they say, not much wider than his nose.

John Rake meanwhile, peeved that he was upstaged by the demiurge, passes to the attack—

"Are you now or have you ever been a member of the black race?"

Before Slim can answer, J. Rake drives on. "You are — are you not — the product of miscegenation?"

"This is called black baiting," the General says, waving a dismissing hand toward John. "I allow it now and then. It clears the air. Now then. Do you have any questions for me?"

Tom and Slim nod and Tom goes first—

"Is it true that emulation recapitulates adulation?"

"True."

And Slim, "Why is the favorite model of officers the braggart and inane?"

"True."

And Tom, "Can you tell the folks back home when this war will end?"

"The answer is classified."

And Slim, "Can I go to the little boys' room now?"

Johnny Demogorgon jumps to his feet. "That's it! That's it!" he shouts, thumping the table with his fists.

Slim picks up a handful of loose tacks and throws them at John D. Johnny leaps upon the table. The demiurge straddles the air. Tom throws *him* a pot of tea. Slim empties an inkwell all over the General's pretty maps.

Ironcoffin tears out a handful of grass and stuffs it in his mouth, fuming. "Stop! stop!" He spits. "By the gawds! I'll have you shot! I'll have you flayed!"

Prudence brings everyone to a position of calm and composure.

"Now, let's get on with it, shall we?" says the General. "I have been receiving hourly reports on your movement since you entered the Dram.

"That's a lie!" Demogorgon shouts.

"For Pete's sake," Ironcoffin says, turning to the demiurge, "Chew on him awhile, will you?"

The demiurge complies and therein lies the whole reason why Johnny Demogorgon spoke no more.

"Tell us, General," says Tom, "are you planning an attack on Dram?"

"Planning? It's afoot. Look it, look it." In his mind he hops up and down and claps his hands, but on the outside he makes a sweeping gesture over the mapboard with a polished hand—

"First," he says, "I am sending a small commando detachment of doctors. Inside of a week — give or take — they're going to have the town forming long lines, treating the citizens like imbeciles, laying diseases on them, the works.

"And then — *then* — the main stroke will come from the south: a cloud of lawyers with their load. I think that'll pack it in.

"I may not be General Douglas Jackson, but never before has there been such economy of force. I expect the mop up operation can be handled with a handful of surgeons to rearrange the parts.

"Well, what do you think?"

"Has the town offended you so much that you would thus inflict upon it a fate worse than death?"

"Hurt is the word."

"Still, there are some nice things in the town."

"Nice is right."

"Then it's hopeless—"

"Hopeless. A good word."

"When is the attack due to begin?"

"The answer is still classified."

"General, is there a medal in this for you?"

"Well, to that I can say, yes. A big cardboard box full of diapers.

"Okay, gentlemen. That about kicks it. Report *that* to the nation, it's your only duty."

His limousines have been brought up. He gets in the first; his mastiff gets in the second; his cane in the third; the demiurge in the fourth; the fifth is occupied by a regurgitated Johnny Demogorgon. The caravan, trailing dust, tears up the dirt road heading into the valley, away from Dram.

In no time at all the limousines reappear out of their own cloud of dust, with everybody carrying ice cream cones, an early victory celebration.

Premature? Unmistakably, collections of white smocks are seen to move on the town, furtive, detectable by the trace of formaldehyde they leave in the air. Who could care that the Dram be scattered into oblivion?

The General is relaxed, his mouth has grown; he kicks the demiurge in the groin and laughs. Tom had had in another time a certain admiration for great generals, Belisarius certainly, Hannibal—.

They form a column, a ceremonial procession really, with Tom and Slim beside the General, and the others bringing up the rear. A hunchback with one arm holds the mastiff's cone.

"I like you boys," the General says. "I'm kind of sorry now I didn't get you any ice cream."

He pushes the air away with his cane.

"What did you do before you became reporters?"

"I was an electrician," Tom says.

"And you?"

"An electrician," says Slim.

"That's interesting."

John Rake Demogorgon, nonchalant behind his cone, comes too close to the conversation: Slim slaps the elbow from which the lower arm extends to the hand holding the ice cream at the entrance to the mouth. The Rake falls back, with little wisps of smoke curling out of his ears, gnashing his teeth.

The demiurge has paused in the eating of his cone, an eye on the policy advisor. Now that he is standing, it can be seen the demiurge is only five feet tall and nearly as wide, without a neck; it is a roguish head, with skin the color of mottled blood, and with corkscrew hair; almost noseless; twin and tiny dots function as a nose above a cavernous oral orifice that opens nearly from ear to ear. He eats the dead.

Ironcoffin giggles. "I like you boys. I really do. But don't knock the John too hard. I like him too. Right, John boy?

"He's very useful to me. He knows who to kill. Tell em the legend of Hersuit, John boy. Tell em."

So John Rake Demogorgon speaks the legend of Hersuit as he is bid—

"Once upon a time, in the village of Hersuit, near the Place of Darkness, on the edge of nowhere, there lived a little dreamy girl, a lovely child, a reincarnated enchantress she must have been, so lovely pure and disarming in her ways, such gentle smile, and quietude of eye, she cast a spell. The good citizens of Hersuit looked upon her with a mixture of suspicion and derision, they being an evil smelling lot.

"The children came and rose, and generations passed, hunting mushrooms, and she remained. The derision of yesteryear turned into contempt when what began to issue from her mind were tiny ants that went about town with small alms buckets collecting bread crumbs and bureaucrats. But later the suspicion turned into terror as from her mind emerged creatures of one-eye with worm-like bodies and bulging heads, swaying forth and engulfing.

"The town is gone now, a semidesert place, not much different from Los Angeles, with mounds crisscrossed by the tunnels of the worms. And every spring, after the rains, priests bring their congregations and biochemists their students and all pray after their fashion."

Ironcoffin claps. "Well done, my John, well done!" And to Tom and Slim, "Now what's so special about that, you ask? I'll tell you. It's this. At the time, the John was in Hersuit — that's right, he was there — minding his trade, being phrenologist, palmist and astrologer, consultant to the town.

"He told them all to kill this young creature, even *before* the ants, but they had this idea, he says, about showing mercy to sweet things. To show mercy for the innocent is a weakness. You see what they do to you?

"Anyway, that's when I hired him."

A camp follower runs up with a gun which the General shoots off without even breaking the measure of his stride.

"This action against the Dram," he says, "is nothing more than a punitive expedition. You understand that. I know you do.

"I like you boys— you've got fine minds and nice hats. Why do you carry them like that under your arm, like Abraham Jefferson? Never mind, never mind.

"As you can see, I'm in a pensive mood today. When the Dram has been reduced to a babble we shall move in there and wipe it clean. It's not every day I get a chance to bare my soul, you understand?

"The boys and I were talking the other day— I don't mean John and the runt here, I mean men like me, my compeers, my equals. My position was, I'm not sure about the neutron bomb. I mean I have my reservations. I know it would suit a bunch of us to kill every blessed thing that lives, forever. Or mutate em. What do you think a three legged rabbit with five eyes would feel like? Damn!— and would you want to *eat* it? What I don't like is the idea of killing everything but leaving all the properties standing. That bothers me. That bothers me a lot.

"I mean, for me, the sight of rubble is — how can I say? — exhilarating, patriotic. Much as it is, I might add, for my good friend General "Gar" Godsalrite Armbuster. He likes to kill, with foretaste and good intentions asunder he pulverizes the ailing throng or the idle intention.

"Anyway, that's the big argument back at the office. You'll always find some types to argue the latest craze. But I'll tell you, the type that bugs me is the type that says it makes no difference, just another tactical option. Listen. To pound the unsuspecting enemy back into the Stone Age, to lay waste for a thousand years, to tear up his children and the children of his children, to dye the earth with their blood— these are things a man can enjoy and they are charlatans who pretend to condemn us."

The demiurge taps his forehead with one of his three-fingered hands. "The wondrous thing most sublime which is rapine and murder and mayhem."

"I'm glad we've come to total war," the General continues after smiling fondly at the demiurge. "I mean at least that concept is acquired and we're finished — in reality, which is where it counts — we're finished with that crap about the sanctity of the person and privileged sanctuaries. Annihilation of the breed is the name of the game, boys. Now wouldn't you know there's always some sucker to think *somebody* will make it, right? Make it to what?"

"Make it over to his grave and close the lid?" Slim suggests.

The General laughs. A white foam has gathered at the corners of his mouth, he is panting; his cane shakes; Johnny D. and the demiurge are weeping at the eloquence. Thus has a Master of the Dank summoned the wind of death and spoke of mindless slaughter and ruination; the grass turned brown and insects fell to silence and birds ceased to pass overhead.

"A general is nothing more than the instrument of his masters," Ironcoffin says gravely.

"That is a truth not only of your profession," says Tom.

He and Slim have donned their hats.

"I should have known," Tom says. "I should have known."

"It is regrettable that you did not leave when I went for ice cream," says General Edward Hail Drepanon, called Ironcoffin. "As you can well imagine, John Demogorgon has recommended your assassination. You know too much. It's true, you should have known. A man of my dimensions only bares his soul to the dead."

Do the campfollowers begin a litany? Do plumes of malodorous incense rise? Nay: that bastard death prefers the awe struck, and so they stand, the company, in the background, like a still photograph, with the whites of their eyes strangely prominent in the brown and yellow air.

Meanwhile, as though all this had been discussed on a street corner, a crowd has gathered silently. There are men here, young and old; and women, in all manner of sizes and shapes; and children with mud pies and baseball bats and rusty bayonets; and baby carriages, and old boots; and staring eyes that have understood.

"A warlock!" Johnny D. gasps, pointing at Tom.

And Tom laughs. It's clear John Rake has not understood.

In olden times, in other days, the group — General and demiurge, John and dog — would have been turned to statues upon the hill, frozen in perpetuity, and the hill would have become barren and the air about grown heavy with madness so that the people would have known to avoid the place and visit it not and spit upon the memory of it.

And later still, the foursome would have been planted up to the knees, with the cane between them, and a ring of flowers laid around them and salt sprinkled over them, and they who have been stuck would fume and crackle and burn. And so in part it is today. They are planted and the cane is placed and the flowers laid and people walk past with burning eyes until the planted ones wither and turn black and then to ash and disappear.

The liberation from a tyranny — even the tyranny of a vision — is a time for exultation, a time of joy and feasting, the land of folk dream pleasure and honey, drink and song; wine and merry wives; you have not seen the face of happiness; and even the screwing going on behind the windbreak is no longer a route to forgetfulness, it is a remembering, the gentle touch of being human. The songs are new. The name of the party was: one day the gods shall die, and man shall inherit the garden forever.

The Crossing of the Often

It was the soldiers who gave Tom and Slim each, for the road, a slab of bacon and powdered eggs and flour; others gave fruit and flowers and wind blown kisses. The journey presses them like a sadness. What are those hills there? and those beyond? do we head north or east? and home?

Someone warned them to go neither to Whipapenny nor Shatterbrain. Others said the woods are filled with ancient dread. The land is ill... One spoke of the Sludge River. Another of the place where whistles blow at periodic intervals and men live to the rhythm of mounted dials. It is, some think, a new religion— the secret pulse of a dozen numbers, a Pythagorean magic, creating in its believers an illusion of measure and order; clearly a case of mass insanity.

They walked down the road until they came to the River Often and crossed over it, at a footbridge there. It was early evening on the other side, so they gathered stones and faggots to make a fire and warm their buns.

They were squatting, rubbing their hands over the fire, when they saw her, a child, nearby— why had they not seen her before? She stood in the rushes, not much taller than them, gazing into the black silence of the Often. Her black hair follows the line of the bent head, exposing only a part of the cheek, a small patch of skin the color of cream; a nose that is not yet fully formed, half-lowered lids— Slim leapt forward as she seemed to fold into the River (so swift, so unalterably swift that gesture).

Tom rushed to the right toward the figure of an old man stepping from behind a tree. His eyes are set where the cheekbones are on other men, his lower lip hangs loose. And as Tom neared the other released a powerful odor of damp and mildew and his chest swelled and he showed yellow teeth.

"Let me touch you," the old man pleaded, "let me touch you." It was the voice of despair disguised as sadness, harbinger of death.

They fought with quarter staff, its thud and smack cracking in the gathering dark.

Slim, meanwhile, felt a hand pass him in the dark of the Often and grabbed it and pulled it to him and then they surfaced and he held her chin and swam a sidestroke back to shore. He carried her, his eyes trembling on her, warming her against him. She felt so cool and silent, so far away from his distress. Tom watched for the better part of the night his friend with the child gathered to him, watched him rock her to and fro and mumble what could not be understood. So he had beaten back despair, he had cracked the skull of the old swine— too late, the other had had the tenacity of defeat, till it ran off. The mold and mildew though kept their odors in the air and crept to the outskirts of the fire and waited there.

From a few yards away it was just a fire, and a man standing, and another sitting on his heels with a child folded in his arms. And beyond lay the darkness of the river swishing at its banks, and further back the hills without lights, dark sleeping giants with their backs curled against the night, and over all, the sky with its points of light receding, perhaps forever, into the obscurity. What can be said? It is the way of death and sadness.

He had missed her there in the dark of the river. The hand had slipped from him. He had swum and swum and plunged and groped like a blind man; there had been only turbulence there, of the liquid of the river.

In the morning she was gone. The fire was dead. Slim stood beside the river and whispered, how does one bid farewell? Not now. Not ever. Flow gently sweet Often. They gathered their belongings and trudged on up the road. Such are the ways of victory and defeat.

Tom is compelled to cover the silence with words. He tells the story of the man who embezzled himself. He put himself into a suitcase, picked himself up and took off. Years later the constabulary found the suitcase in a locker of an abandoned railroad station, with a moist and empty blue serge suit in it. The man was never seen nor heard from again.

He tells the story of Caddy Sawbucks, the creeping lizard; and the one about the doctor whose business was going to pot until he went to the local pharmaceutical industry and purchased a coffin full of coughs.

And also of the man who shot his wad at the circus, throwing baseballs at a woman's fan. He came home to a wife in ecstasy preparing to divorce him. She had met her destiny that afternoon, while working at the circus, having men throw baseballs at her fan. A preacher told him that one, to illustrate the evil of lying.

"Shall I tell you the history of Moredekaibo Halftit?"

"You might as well."

"Moredekaibo Halftit," Tom says, "was the first delegate to arrive for the constitutional convention at Philadelphia. Halftit was refused a seat on the grounds that it could not be believed this was his real name. Pseudonyms were grounds for automatic disqualification in those days.

"Two years later the Halftit Rebellion broke out. It was widely believed at the time that the Rebellion was led by women with only half their share of mammary glands. This in turn led to the first exposition of the theory of conspiracy of foreign elements invading a contented body politic. It followed that this was the first recorded attempt to undermine motherhood. (A later view of the conspiracy had both tits replaced first by glass bottles, then by plastic ones.) Halftit, despairing of having the opportunity to advance his cause — or even state it — retired into anonymity on a farm in eastern Kentucky."

Tom's voice died.

The sun had risen above the eastern edge of the world. The light shines on the bones of the living and warms them. The jackals of the mind flee back toward the night.

Hepatica, anemone and daffodil beckon from the side of the road, stretching away into the fields. Fruit trees are in the valley. There is a cow or two. It is placid, bucolic, a place where some had thought once to settle down and build a house with their own hands.

"Well, friend?" says Tom, looking toward the distant places.

And Slim nods, ready.

Over yonder lies a mountain. Isn't that where wise men live so the travail of the world will not disturb their meditation? And is it not possible — merely possible — they know a way, or have heard of one...

Friends, Romans and Origins

They meet an old man on the road, a scholar, as witness a leather pouch or satchel full of papers; sloped of shoulder and back, a diminutive fellow with an ancient pair of pince-nez that keeps falling off his nose and dangling by his cravat soiled with mustard and succotash.

His wife, being his chief devotee and guardian, is a huge woman of scowling mien. She carries their one suitcase. Feeling her husband threatened she has been known to wrap him in her arms and shout above his head to her vision of his assailants. She joined the feminist movement thirty years ago. She is presently campaigning to change the word hysterectomy to hersterectomy as a way of making that operation more palatable.

They have a son, — not present here — an advertising man, who has convinced himself his ads are poetry. It is called a Sustaining Illusion. He makes the old man sad. The parents rarely see him.

All in all it has not been the best of lives for the scholar.

Yet at the sight of the two young men (he thought at first they were part of a carnival act), his eyes grew bright and his cheeks flushed again. Did they remind him of his former students?

He inquired of the weather whence they came, and what books they had read, and whether the roads were paved and astrology were in vogue, and if the women were all beautiful and free.

"The most of them," said Slim, "are like here, constipated shrews."

"Are the men fools and blowhards?"

"Many, yes ma'am."

"Male chauvinist pigs?"

"Many like those too, yes ma'am."

"At least you're honest."

The old man laughed, a pleasant jingle, avoiding the clouds gathering in the eyes of his wife.

It was this pleasant atmosphere, this unexpected camaraderie, as the Irish say, of the road, that prompted the old man to pass the walking time by telling them of Rome, ancient mercantile empire, of ill repute.

"It is said," he began, "that Aeneas lugged his Father over hill and dale from Troytown to the land of the Etruscans. It sounds good, full of filial piety, and what later would become Roman gusto and remorseless devotion, until one remembers such a trek to be — overland — several thousand miles, peopled along the way with many races and police forces who, if nothing else, would have at least stayed the pair a while, to puzzle over a strong young man in loincloth carrying a wounded old man to a hospital so far away. Would they not at least have questioned his motives vis a vis the old man? Granted that the sons wish to visit upon their fathers the pains of the long march. Granted also that he was strong, and even: his motives pure. Still, the fable collapses against the commonplace. I mean, how could he stop to cook supper with an old man peering from over his shoulder, threatening, at any moment, to topple over into the soup?

"Forego cooking then? No man can walk 2,000 miles without a meal. Nor can it be assumed that Aeneas was a god in disguise, because the Romans, unlike the Greeks, had no gods that indulged in transmogrification.

"So this trip bears closer examination. The later Roman taste for converting their enemies into slaves (among whom galley slaves), befits a people seeking retribution for an ancient humiliation.

"The Romans were strong on humiliation. Remember Caesar's caveat? There is a humiliation of your enemy past which it is imprudent to let him live. This approach of mine is attested to by a psychohistorian, according to whom the resemblance of the Imperial Scepter to a protruding Navel comes from the fact that Augustus' mother, Agrippina,

Caesar's wife, was his stepmother: that he realized the arcane impossibility of ever being or having been attached to her navel and therefore created *tutti frutti* a surrogate navel— the Imperial Scepter. It would rule a thousand years, don't forget. Be that as it may and getting back to the ancient humiliation about galley slaves, it is clear the Romans were Rowmen: I suggest they were themselves galley slaves, in the dim Doric age of Hellas.

"This is confirmed by another etymology— the name Aeneas comes from Akneesass, which in turn is a singularly uncomfortable phenomenon known to all galley slaves of the Ancient World. It must be recalled also that the Grecian trireme was probable even more uncomfortable than the Roman variety, and therefore the phenomenon even more uncomfortable, especially to a people with anal-retentive characteristics. Aeneas probably acquired the nickname for complaining more than most.

"Now recall that Akneesass (or Aeneas) departed Troytown at its fall. Visualize the moment: the burning towers, the wooden horse crashing around, stomping on the natives, Hector dead, the same for Troilus and old Pandar, and Cryseyde; the screams and moans and smoke, the fits of the dying, the hapless heads upon the spikes of the conquerors; all pandemonium and mayhem.

"And our hero, Aeneas, who, during the months of siege, filed away at his ankle chains, is free now, as are his fellow Rowmens. They mount a small revolt on the ship that contains them, slay their Grecian guards, cut moorings, and set sail and oar for somewhere else across the Mare Nostrum (nos, being Nuit, or Night, and Mare, sea, hence the Night Sea, whence the English, Nightmare): set sail, I say, upon the Nightmare, the Sea of Night (later renamed by more cosmopolitan Romans, the Place between land: Mediterranean), until they came to the Tiber thence upward to the Etruscan village in the basin of the Seven Hills, to the foundation of Rome.

"Now I ask you, with such questionable beginnings would you not also resort to fable— even to say Rome was really founded by so remote a conjunction as the coming to the place by a couple of brothers brought up by wolves? and the sudden death by plague or other convenience of all Etruscans? And later, when you come into the money, wouldn't you hire an official historian to doctor up the text? make everybody smell good?

"I visited in Thebos once the remains of a trireme. You could still detect after these several thousand years the odor of sweat.

"But to get back to the matter. If you had savaged the Etruscans, like we did the Indians, would you want some explanation, eh? eh?

"Think. We don't teach our kids about slavery, we teach them what Strom Calhoun had to say on the matter, or that Tom and George freed theirs, after they were dead. Is that a joke? is it? for god's sake?"

His wife comforts him, "There, there, old bloke, cheer up. Show these 'ere gents some cheek, me lovely." It is her habit to fall thus into an older dialect when she is moved.

"And look," he says, "once in Rome, what happens? They take to booty hunting, gun running, peddling hash and horse, letting the law run amuck among the poor—"

"Speaking of law," says Tom, "I'm sure you've heard of the *neva neva* case, pronounced knee-va? It's a famous Roman case, reported by Tacitus, in which *amicus curiae* (friends of the clergy) briefs were filed tending to prove that what separated — and thereby sets above all — the Roman from all others was the location of his brains in his knees."

The old man laughs, it has the sound of defiance against everything that has wanted to destroy him.

"Ahh," he says, "I am so pleased to have run into you boys— you've made my day. What am I saying? My week, my month!

"Of course I've heard of the *neva neva*. It is the first recorded case of the use of the *spurioso grosso* doctrine, namely, the grossly spurious, a formidable lawyer's tool. There was also in the same case — as I am sure you know — *combinatio sub implementa*, Roman for a nice deal that can't be implemented, to be distinguished from *combinatio sub rosa*, which is a combination under the roses, a euphemism for smelly deals under sweet words.

"In Rome," he raises his index finger, "there was no social, political or economic question which did not ultimately degenerate into a case before the courts. The law was not used to subvert the rational, the law was the subversion, a condition it has never overcome. Whatever it grants of what is sane must be wrenched from it, as from the head of a madman. It is no accident that the greatest Roman god was Law— the legate he was called, i.e., he who ate legs—"

"As you can see," his wife breaks in, "Henry loves to talk. What he has to say is bullshit, of course— but it is such an uncanny demonstration of erudition, don't you agree? —My Henry," she says, fondly, drawing a custodial arm around him.

His monologue lasted much of the time it took to cross the valley. And now they have come to a fork in the road. He says his name by the way is Henry Hurlbutt. She was born Martha Lou Smothers. Take a look at my new home, says he, handing Tom a pair of binoculars fished out of the leather pouch.

"Dissent is permissible," Henry resumes, "providing it's in the right direction. I was hounded from the University."

"Retired, Henry, retired. We mustn't be bitter now, must we?"

Sometimes he calls her, my svelte. She calls him, my little jive ass humdinger.

"And where are you boys heading?" Henry asks.

"We heard," says Slim, "there was a wiseman in the hills—"

"He is a dummy," says Mizz Hurlbutt. "Believe me. He teaches nothing but male bullshit. Like the rest of them, an imbecile.

"Well, come, Henry. We'll leave these boys to their devices."

"I feel a cold coming for me," Henry says, with a little smile, taking the glasses back from Tom and returning them to his satchel. He raises a hand to them and turns to follow Martha Lou toward the balance of his destiny.

Through the glass Tom — and Slim after him — had seen the sign: Purse, Retirement Village. It looked like a pleasant sarcophagus. Old people were lined up on the porches. Some sat, some fell off their rockers, others nodded or counted beads. A bunch played croquet on the village green, but it was too far to hear the mallet slap and the mumble of voices.

And all around at tables everywhere others played cards— canasta, and two handed solitaire, and gin rummy, and two men holed up on a porch roof played cribbage, others had passed on to hearts and fish and Old Maid.

Horatio the Wise

An Indian could have read a history of the place from the signs on the high road— the ruts of tires of heavy vehicles, the moccasins of mountain men, the boots of lumberjacks, the shoes of the curious, the sandals of the religious. When did strip mining decapitate the first prominence? Tom and Slim pause amidst the obvious traces of the giant machines that ripped away the earth. The downslope is a river of slag, releasing an acid waste with every rain, percolating into the ground water, reappearing somewhere no doubt, to poison wells, before passing into the universal cesspool, the sea.

It isn't the silence of the dead that weighs here, like it does in cemeteries and old battlefields, it is the menace of death. And for how long does it remain a menace? 200 years? more? They remind themselves to take heart. There are places where the Earth has received radioactive wastes: there the use of the ground is prohibited forever.

"Damn," says Slim. They hurry over the broken ground.

Some, back home, had dreamed of mutations that would produce animals that could eat slag, bacteria that would eat petroleum drifting on the oceans, consume radioactive waste and excrete carrots, reminiscent of the amoeboid mass that fed off the sewers of Metropolis until it burst from its confines and would have consumed the city but for the timely intervention of Superman.

Coal and oil and natural gas are the remains of the ancient dead, rising to haunt the living. An environmentalist thought the fumes of the dead so boiled inside the brains of the living they have produced a time enamored of death. And the animist tribes were right to fear the power of the dead. What strange fantasies men weave to explain away the historical errors of others.

Six hours later they are two thousand feet above the slag and decide to call it a day. They pull their hats down and lean against the coarse bark: it has a friendly living warmth. There are no ghosts on the mountain. The mountains were in ancient times a place for the gods, those projections of man's spirit, dominating him like alien things set against him; the gods tolerated no wandering human spirits in their midst. Ghosts haunted the arbors, the glades, the plains. There are tales of men who hear the voices of the dead, which has been found particularly useful in archeology for locating the burial place of a dead Indian woman and her child, caught in a mudslide; or describing the round houses and burial customs of Cro-Magnon.

Tom says he thinks they must be somewhere on the east coast. There isn't a mountain here above 8,000 feet. Were they on the west coast would they not be in the shadows of the Tetons? the Cascades? the white forbidding silence of Mount Shasta? And if they got a compass and took a bearing? They could head toward the coast, find the cities! the friendly ugly faces!

Slim reminds him they are in paradise— and what makes him (Tom) think the hills they've gone over aren't buried cities? They could be buried cities. Isn't half the known world covered with cities? sometimes six layers deep?

This kind of reflection brings Tom to his senses. It must be the heady mountain air that makes a man go nuts with the desire to break into his former cage. He looks around. The wind stirs in the pines.

There was a time when a man (an intelligent man) could speak of mountain people in terms of free spirit and will and determination; the sheep lived below on the plain. Now the men of the plains can approach the mountain and reduce it, a sterile conquest, perhaps. For it is written (in a book) that to keep the plains fertile, keep the highlands in forest. Bethink you of the Phoenicians who zapped the cedars of Lebanon, like the Romans ate Sicily. In less than a hundred years the Americans devastated three quarters of their soil. What rapacity. And to those who ask, what cunning do the gods employ to slay those creatures? The answer used to be, madness. Mostly madness. Only now the madman has the power to take the world down with him.

The rain is not wise. The wind does not cry in the darkness. It is no longer possible to speak of the endurance of the mountains. They sleep.

In the morning they climb another 4,000 feet. They do not tarry in the ruins of Rundle. The legend has it that on the consecrated ground of the House of Futhorc the runster, the people spat upon a rune of his that offended their sensibilities; he called down the fire and wrath upon them and when nothing came of it the people heaved him from the mountain and sacked the place and burned it to the ground and went their way.

It is not far above this that they come upon Nicholas von Lumen Slabberdathy. He sits athwart the path on a concrete slab, gathering piles. His head swings up and away from the comic book in his lap, and he taps his forehead with his fingers, saying, oh wow, oh wow. And then his head swings down again and he mumbles other things incomprehensible, and up again, this time tapping the image on the open page and saying, oh wow, oh wow.

His hair and eyebrows have been bleached to the color of wet plaster; his eyes are pale blue and bloodshot red. He lives inside a sheepskin coat.

A good five minutes pass before he notices the pair in tophats and tails, like twins they are to him, or a double image, brown of eye and hair like a hundred million others, neither tall nor short.

His voice has the kind of breathless excitement used by acid freaks, and all he says is, "Who are you?"

"My name is Tom. This is Slim."

Nick just turns the comics to them and taps the page. It's Batman against six or seven of the henchmen of Tsk-Tsk or the Razy Ghoul. This is the new Batman, dark and towering figure, strong, agile beyond belief, a true nemesis to his prey, unlike the runt of yore whose fists made sounds like pow, kapow and boppo; who never smiled, and talked through his teeth even to his friends the police.

"We heard," says Tom, "there was a wiseman—"

"Oh wow," Nick says, touching his forehead. "There's no wiseman up here, man."

"No?"

Nick shakes his head. "Just this old mackerel who spits a lot. Now don't get me wrong, I'm not knocking him. He's beautiful, man, beautiful. But I know the truth, man, the real groove on reality, man. It's all up here—" He taps his temple with one finger. "But folks can't hear, you dig? Like I'm talking to you now, man— and you don't understand, cause you think I'm using words you understand, man. Your head's someplace else, man. That's where it's at. Right?"

He rocks himself from side to side, saying, "You look at the Batman here, you think, man, that's a gas, that guy's got the gig— dressed in drag like that, for halloween." He stops rocking. "Right? You're wrong. He's got it all up here, man." He taps his temple again like he did the first time.

"Like he's working out his karma, man. He's doing his thing, man, and you think he's working for the police. Right? Oh shit, man, you two are out of it."

His eye falls on an image of the cowled crusader and he cocks his head and rocks it, oh wow, oh wow.

They used to say, over such experiences, I groove on that cat; now they say, that turkey turns me on. In those days, about the time of grooving on the cat, there was a man who thought it less demeaning to play a part in a porno film than work in a factory. Now it is known he would simply not die as fast.

They step around von Lumen Slabberdathy, engrossed already in a peripheral psychic exploration of Iron Man, a sentimental type who carries on an endless conversation with himself about lost loves and his failure to waylay opportunities while he raps together the heads of his enemies.

They climb another 500 meters, almost straight up and come abruptly unto a plateau. The mountain goes on. But here in the middle of the scene, crossed legged, in the asana of meditation, an old man sits, facing east, into a sun too large for man to eat.

His hair is white, his beard is white; the air barely ruffles the lacey material into which he is enfolded. To the rear, in the rock face, is the entrance to a cave much like the one next to Nicholas below.

Tom and Slim come forth on cat feet to within a yard of the seated figure and then they squat. How does one begin? Master? Sir? Ah-hum?

It is awkward. His eyes are barely open. For all they know the old man may not even be here, out of his body someplace, on an astral journey.

"It's not as though we were curiosity seekers," Slim says in self-defense.

Tom agrees. So they peer closely at the face, hoping to wake it up. But it doesn't move, meditating like a stone.

"When one goes on an astral journey," Slim wonders, "does the body turn into plaster?"

"Improbable hypothesis."

"Then look," says Slim, laying a finger upside the nose of the old man and pushing.

"Wait—" Tom raises a hand. He heard somewhere that if you touch a body while the spirit is out on a visit, the body shatters like an eggshell and you have another lost soul on your hands.

The figure topples over.

"A plaster model," Slim says, coming to his feet, disgusted.

"Hey! what the hell do you think you're doing?" cries the voice of a man hurrying out of the cave.

"Goddam! Five years he sat there without a body touching him. Who the hell are you?"

"My name is Tom. This here is Slim."

"Mine's Horatio."

He is a short and stocky man in coveralls and the boots of a lumberjack.

They shake hands.

"Thunderation," Horatio says, "you caused me a fright. Folks've been coming up here for years and they just kneel in front of Jacob here. That's what I call him— don't rightly know his true moniker, we were never introduced. Like I say, they kneel and say their piece and then they leave. Seem perfectly satisfied."

"You mean there's never been a Jacob?"

"Oh sure, sure. I'm passing by here five years back and find this feller dressed skimpy, thin as a rail, half-starved to death. He was a wiseman all right. Been up here so long, didn't even remember his own name.

"He paid this other fellow, Nick Slabface, to guard the path below, don't ask him questions, keep out the folks; a thousand quid, near 5,000 bucks at the time."

"He's still there."

"That so? —Anyhow, Jacob here he couldn't hang on no more, gave up the ghost, like folks say, he died. I think, no how, he lost his marbles way before. He'd look like this," — he makes his eyes as big as possible — "square in the face, and couldn't see me."

"So where do you come in?" asks Slim.

"I made the plaster stature of Jacob here and set him on the mat and let him pray. What harm, I figure? You get a religious bugger come up here and think it was for nothing, no telling what he'd do. Meanwhile, I got me a perfect stash. Who's going to be the wiser? And where's the hurt?"

"What are you hiding from?" Tom asks.

"Not exactly hiding, friend. For the peace and quiet. I had a friend up here with me, trained bears then set em loose to catch businessmen when they come asporting, and lick their feet till they went nuts then set em loose."

Slim shakes his head. "I hate to say it but it's a hell of a thing to inflict on bears."

"Thought so myself, but he was a good friend. He had an especial hatred for the type, understand— thought them the cause of the world being upside down.

"Course they're not the cause. The world stinks by its lonesome. The bears got wise to my friend though, so they ate him. They may not have taken kindly to the smelly feet."

He was born, this Horatio, Theobold Furnlucci. He grew to be short, stocky, to wear only coveralls and lumberjack boots and beige and brown checkered shirts. No one remembers when he did not look like an elf: small eyes, low cheekbones (level with the lower edge of his nostrils), a grin. He gave no reason, around the age of 30, for assuming the name Horatio. A year later he stuffed a pair of coveralls with rags. There was an autopsy, the pathologist, a forensic specialist, pronounced him dead. Horatio's line was dead, there would be no succession, he had been himself his only remaining relative. He said once, I know the valley people, they're high on death. It seemed sufficient reason to withdraw.

"You gents don't strike me as the type needs the services of a feller like Jacob here. Plus you touched him. Religious folk would have crossed themselves and eaten a little dirt. You heading north?"

"Well, we heard there was a wiseman up here," Tom says. "We thought — in a way, we hoped — he would know of a way out of this place."

"Sure you don't mean to get off the mountain, you just come up. You want to get off the world? I recall some other feller came up here, wanted to climb to the peak up there and reach up and grab the sky and yank himself over. You don't mean like that?"

"Not exactly. We were thinking maybe— a road, a door."

"No doors here, gents. No roads either. There's the path you came up. There's another, heading east—" He points down toward the valley that stretches to the horizon.

"Course, there was a time folks came up thinking they could fly. Some freak down there was telling them, it's all right, trust me. Right off the edge." He shakes his head. "World full of loons."

Clearly, it is hopeless. Is Horatio wise? There is no way out via a path a road a door. Who was it said, all roads don't have to lead to Boston? Surely another piece of wisdom lies in that.

The path down the mountain, heading east, avoids the slag.

"Be thankful," says Tom, "for small blessings."

"You head east then?"

"East it is."

"Merry weather to you," says Horatio.

"Dead men hail no taxis," Slim says, raising a hand in farewell.

"That's the truth," Horatio says.

They have regained their confidence. They will not admit despair. There isn't a prison built that men have not been able to get out of. And besides, life is still here. This is still it. Only here are there mornings like this— only here, among the living, is the light a music, a joyous rage, rising in the pristine air. It cuts the breath away. Men have drunk the light and felt the force of what lives. It seems impossible that the species will not last.

So they turn down the path that leads to the valleys in the east.

PART TWO

The Feast of Anapaest

Once upon the plain they shuffle through rose light, hats on their heads, hands in their pockets. Tom fills the time with anecdotes from the life of Marvin Kutemovsky, affectionately dubbed the Ax, chief surgeon at the giant medical facilities of Permutation-on-Hudson.

His early career was devoted largely to alleviating the sufferings endemic to obesity. It was not known at the time that *Homo sapiens obesus*, no longer merely a sport, was about to be elevated to the level of a new species. He wired the mouths of the corpulent so they could not eat, he removed portions of their stomachs, their intestines. It was while poking around inside somebody one day that he found the thymus: it was such a tiny thing, so he, thinking big as always, made the natural assumption that a thing so small could have no value. Thymus snipping became the craze. It must be said to his credit that the relation between this gland and the immunological system was not yet known. Meanwhile he continued to perform thousands upon thousands of *saddlebaggi fatectomies* (removal of subcutaneous fat from butt and thigh).

But it was around the age of 40, at the height of his powers, that he revealed the true magic of his scalpel. In compliance with what was at the time the order from higher up about hopping to it, he went around amputating one leg from the gullible. And thus did he exemplify the old saw that the pursuit of private gain serves the common good.

He went on to invent the thumbnail transplant, placed at the left armpit so this could be scratched without disturbing the hands. Following upon this a major drug company proposed to precoat the nail with a carcinogenic infection inhibitor. And a major auto company planned new car sales around it as a new safety device that would only modestly effect the cost of the vehicle.

It was he who presided at the famous Operation Triocular, wherein, after shaving of the head, the subject had a third eye implanted one centimeter above the right ear so that, standing busy at the cash register, he could continue to observe the sly shoppers.

Finally, according to Monk, in *Encyclopedia of Medical Moneymakers*, Marvin is credited with the discovery, or perhaps only the systematized investigation of two well known syndromes, viz.— Cabezza di dottore and Crapknee.

The pathogenic features of Cabezza di dottore (also known as Caboche de docteur) are dependence, helplessness, transvitae weakness, subacute povertosis, generalized proliferating impoverishment, and death.

Crapknee, on the other hand, is an affliction common both to athletes and soldiers. The Crapknee, a true bug, displaces 50 kilos per square millimeter, and by positioning itself atop the kneecap brings such pressure to bear as to be the cause of a noticeable Quiver in the joint of the host. It is incurable. This elevates the Crapknee to one of the true blessings of the healer's art.

It has been rumored by his detractors (no great man is exempt from them) that his true reputation is based upon the fact that in a previous incarnation he had invented for the medical profession, a mechanical bodysnatcher. It is difficult to adjudicate the validity of such a contention, unless of course the reference is to the operating table itself...

"All hail and welcome, sweet males," a voice says, husky and sensuous.

Standing at a gate, which is an opening in a stone wall that stretches out of sight, are three women, the Virgins of the Vestry, so to speak: one holds a handful of tickets, the other a pitcher of water, the third sits with a marked deck of Tarot cards, casting futures upon a table.

They are, all three, dark of hair and eye and lightly dressed and beautiful. None is blonde, for it is said that blondes are silly and that may well be true though a survey might disprove it.

"Wash the dust of the road from your mouths," says she of the pitcher, offering a tumbler to each in turn.

"Take a ticket," says the other, "any ticket."

"I see things in store for you," says the daughter of the Tarot. "Hocus-pocus and mumbo-jumbo, you are two who don't like gumbo— you will find none at our feast."

"Perceptive," Slim nods, approvingly.

The tickets are rectangles of struck gold, embossed with hieroglyphics strange and bold and little men without pantaloons running naked around the edges. So why not stick around?

They tip their hats and pass beneath the smiles of the damsels of the gate into a garden pungent with the odor of cut flowers. The road is made of cobblestones. The tender care of fruit trees to left and right amidst the flower patterns bespeaks a sophisticated husbandry. The road winds between terraced hills where the earth has been turned anew and newly seeded. The wizardry of living things prepares to reemerge from an earth warm and moist again. There was of old a feast of spring where the blood of gods was shed to assure a rejuvenation of the earth. What had begun perhaps as a dark and brutal fever to appease alien forces, became feasts of joy, celebrations of knowledge and companionship with the Earth.

The lady Gertrude, seated on a waystone, rises, dressed in white, gown aflowing. It is not wrong for men to smile at the sight of beautiful women: it should not be wrong for women to smile at the sight of beautiful men.

"You look to me like a fine pair of male chauvinists," she says, smiling, and offering her hand.

"Still," says Tom, for who wants to argue with beauty? "I admire your gardens."

She is pleased at this.

Tom wonders if this world is still under the iron rule of men.

"Back home," he says, by way of exploration, "I had made a pact with myself, to treat women as equals, and to strive for it."

"I have a test of male intentions," she says. "How do you feel about the idea that whatever steps taken toward a humanization of the world are taken by women?"

"Well, ma'am... in my world, it was said that when women got the right to vote there would be an end to war, because they would vote the warriors out of office. It didn't happen. They forgot they wanted equality in a man's world. It's not unusual for a victim to become a strident defender of the master's right. Antigone was willing to die to maintain a tradition. Indian mothers sent their sons to die against the white man."

"Black men," Slim says, "embraced the most retrograde form of the religion that helped keep them in darkness."

Both of them try to look like a pair of professors, following the rumor that these are the least threatening sort of males.

"But the equality of women, in my kind of time, it must come," Tom says. "They also must acquire the right to be taken advantage of, with an impartial hand."

"Also? Who are the others?"

"The men."

"What an evil thought— you make the victims and the butchers one. You are a clever sophist," she says, with such a gentle smile it makes Tom's hands tremble.

"Madam, there is a system of domination for which the domination of men over women is merely another convenience."

"The truth is simpler," she says. "All men are patriarchs."

He waves a hand. "Rather — I think — we are the sons of the patriarch. Some aspire to emulate him, others to destroy him. I knew about a man, in my day, who saw only the guilt of the sons for the death, even the desire for the death, which they brought upon their fathers. Civilization bears the trace of an original patricide—"

"Do you deny that blood and death lie at the foundations of civilizations created by men—?"

"No, madam. But I think guilt isn't the whole story— or that the role of the mother is simply to be an object to possess. There is Saturn, god of time and darkness, on the dining room wall of Goya's house, eating his children. It was the Earth itself, the mother, who tricked him into thinking a rock he was given to swallow was his child. Like a bezoarstone it must have been in his gut.

"But to tell the truth, madam, I'm not too impressed with these brooding cyclic visions of the Greeks, where nothing dies; fallen gods are displaced only' to the wings, where they continue to whine and plot."

"Hey," Slim says, "why did you make so much of Cerberus then, the tetracephalic dog with three tails and snakes all over?"

This dog business breaks the ice, because now they laugh, all three of them.

"So?" Slim persists.

Tom shrugs. "It had seemed a nice way to con her." He says this while looking at the lady and now brings her hand up to his lips to apologize: he thinks their smiles cross in midair and become infatuated.

"In fact," he says, "I much prefer the Norse hymns—"

She takes his arm; he adjusts his pace to hers. Who has not felt the blending? the sense of being one with the world? It is a sense that only comes in pleasure. It is no accident that in sadness the world is alien and hostile, bringing on a feeling of estrangement. It leads to madness and death. Are we all mad?

Pleasure clears faces, they become beautiful. And what is beauty but what is pleasing to the senses? It is a misunderstanding of the senses which makes of that a trivial observation.

"You were saying?"

"I was saying, I much prefer the Norse hymns to life, where the gods are the allies of our species. The story goes that one day the forces of horror and destruction will make a last attempt to consume the world. In the ensuing battle they will be defeated, and the gods will die. We — all of us — will inherit the morning, the light, the Earth."

When will that ever be? he asks himself. How long can we wait? The question sets him brooding. Such are the wiles of sadness, to make a moment of pleasure so brief it fades while it is fresh.

Was the glass of water at the gate a potion? a drug to cloud his mind and create a false euphoria? There are cerebral types who distrust pleasure because they are not smart enough: has he fallen to that? By the path of these reflections he remembers the Amazons. It is said they were warriors who had their right breasts removed to facilitate archery. He had never liked the Princess Diana (also known as Wonder Woman), who came to defend civilization from inside the headquarters of an Intelligence organization. Surely some wise male hoodwinked her into defending a very peculiar set of values— patriotism, philanthropy, and death to the heathens. Certainly that male couldn't be her imbecile sidekick Steve. The oriental charlatan perhaps?

He turns to Slim and is not surprised to see a lady at his side, and he with his head leaned toward her to hear her voice.

"The water—" Tom says.

They have come to the place. It is a basin in the hills; at the bottom lies a rectangle of walls 20 feet high, penetrated on its four sides by massive gates. Men and women, arm in arm, gather from the cardinal points and enter the place and take their seats at a table that nearly spans the length of the enclosure.

The women cease to touch the men. The gates clang shut. All the men rise and mill about like nervous cattle before slaughter. They walk together, giggle nervously, and scan the high walls with their eyes.

There is flute music, accompanied by what may very well be primitive lutes. Then all again are seated and the Lady Herta explains the low-relief sculptures on the doors. They are a history of the humiliation of women. Some scenes depict the binding of the feet to keep them down to doll size; others show the casting of wives into the graves of their husbands, along with their horses and chairs; there are chastity belts and veils, whippings and lapidations; there are rows on rows of witches, the chambers for torturing them, the stakes for burning them; there are women valued in terms of cattle; and those incarnating goddesses to be destroyed; without identity before the law; there are the scenes of infanticide, the crime against the female born, and repudiations; there are girls sold into the stables of emperors and pashas, kings, generals and pimps; and endless hours at the looms; and half pay for work equal to that of a man, like in other days a slave was two-thirds of a person; and behind every great man stands a woman who had nothing better to do.

"Now you will take your places at the table and there will be a feast," says the Lady Herta. "There will be jesters and clowns, stories, music, wine—"

There is at that moment an unveiling at the far end of the court. It is a fertility goddess: her tongue hangs out, her breasts and labia majora are grossly swollen, her arms are rigid at her sides, her legs are barely differentiated. Tom searches for the sacrificial altar, the place of atonement, the signs of blood, the warriors who will cry with him when he is led up.

Food is uncovered. Wine sloshes into glasses. The music rises.

"Speak to me," the Lady Gertrude says, smiling at Tom, gently as before, touching his arm with her hand.

But Tom has turned to Slim to get an opinion.

"What do you think, we are being led to slaughter?"

"You got me."

"What did he say?" asks the lady next to Slim.

"He was reminding me of a line of his, ma'am, which says blonde women have 28 virtues, all the rest have 30 or 31."

"And have you heard," says Tom, leaning backwards so both ladies come into view, "of the rondo vacca? It's named after the habit cows have, on moonlit nights, of forming a circle and dancing. It is often confused with rondo dondo, a Latin vulgarism for dumbbell."

In the background a jester tells of the Anthomyiidae, the tragic tale of love between Rhagoletis and Hylemya. Upon their nuptial night Rhagoletis had to rush out and be destroyed by Zonosemata at the Battle of Tetanops, on the banks of the Longipeenus. Zonosemata then took Hylemya to wife and she begat him a thousand sons...

The Lady Gertrude looks at him. How dark her eyes are, and how troubling. There is no sign of malice there, only a kind of pensive gentleness that unhinges him. The phrase, to fall in love, had always summoned in him images of someone falling off a stool; or in darker moods, a falling, as in failure; and then there was the myth of the fall and the crashing through the ice...

As though again some witch had cast a spell, hexed the day. And tumbling out of memory, out of self-defense, comes the love poem from the Bonnets of Willie the Shake, which he recites almost mournfully—

Be strong in your decay, my sweet.
I do not see the clock that tells the time
Nor will I note your droopy eyes,
Your loss of memory, your painted puss
Or other marks of death; pickled are you
Till time rusts and birds cease to whistle...
And part the second went—
Tired of turmoil I turn to you instead
And find your face drooping around your knees.
How can I still thy salivating In my soup? or girk your smirk—
Were you not buried once?

To be in love a man had to have left his senses. Bizarre. As though we lived with creatures that hunted us in strange ways.

She seems to understand all this without his having used a word. She rises and takes his hand. There is no doubt a physiology, even a physics, of attraction, auras or not, energy fields or not; wrapped still in the mysteries of magic and incantation, secret aphrodisiacs, ground rhinoceros horns and baboon testicles. It would be good to think that those who come together would not forever drift apart.

"It would be horrible," she says, "if the best we could conceive of would be revenge."

And so they begin slowly in each others arms to turn to the music of the flute and the tumble of the clowns, her gown gathering around him. Their eyes are locked. The eyes say everything, even when we do not know how to read them.

And then others join in. The entire rectangle becomes a mass of slowly turning bodies, generating a power even the walls cannot hold, so that on the surrounding hills the flowers burst and even the stone goddess has swallowed her tongue and moved her arms forward like one receives a friend and the legs have separated so that one foot has taken the first step.

In the dim history of the word *wife*, there is wif, meaning woman, meaning breath of air. Some take offense, think woman as insubstantial as the air. But in the mind of Tom the breath of air reminds him of the midwife who long ago breathed into the mouth of the newborn who had not, on his own, begun to breathe, and gave him life, and from this breath it can be said he saw the light. What more is there?

The feast lasted for six days, until even the worms came out to see what the ruckus was about and saw it was only the humans again, making music. The walls have rooms; the wine flows; guitars and banjos replace the flutes and violins; and on the hills the seeds sprout their seed leaves.

Visions of Sugarplums

The time had come to leave. To say they sought a place that was not there, what could that mean? Or mean if they said they sought it because it was the one they knew and did not feel alien there, though it might be changed now beyond recognition, and all your friends dead. They said they needed to go home. She said there was a place for them in Anapaest and things to do. The Lady looked upon him with such sadness he felt his mouth go dry and the surroundings whither and turn gray. She said nothing after that, held out her hand only, and nodded several times when he grasped it with both of his. Slim had walked off a hundred paces to wait. There were no tears on either side. It was early dawn, a chill still lay in the air, the dew was only beginning to shimmer in the light. And then they left. For home...

Slim watched his friend, as they say in a difficult campaign, put one foot in front of the other. Their eyes were ringed with sleeplessness.

He did not know how to tell distracting tales like Tom did, he had no memory for them. He watched the hills come slowly toward them. Each had inherited a quarter staff and a small pouch of food that rested just below the hip slung from a leather strap across the shoulder. The tophats had fallen in the dancing and been crushed so that now they sat askew atop their heads. The long flaps on the swallow tails had been cut. More than ever they looked like a couple of clowns.

"Tell me the tale of hollow eve," Slim said at last. Tom said nothing. It was a tale he had told before.

What is now the eve of hollow (he would say) began in barbarian times. It marked the day the dead drifted in the world. It was fall, fall again, when all things died and the earth grew barren. The folk donned horrid masks to play the parts of demons and restless spirits, and witches came to give them drink and to make peace.

And time passed and the clergy came to put the witches on the rack, and made the ceremony the eve of all hallow, on hallowed ground, to prepare the next day, the day of the holies. For then all the saints would rise to intercede with the alien dead by virtue of the special pleading of the clergy, the exorcists. While God sat on the throne playing solitaire, all the saints would crowd the air, munificent, beneficial, and brush away the ancient dread.

The demon masks remained like some relic whose purpose passed from memory and so what harm to discard them upon children? Who would be concerned with witches — their last nest destroyed in Salemtown by clever men in black smocks — their cats, the whole kit and caboodle of cauldrons and herbs, batwings, wart of frog and testicle of wolf; deformed and cackling, living in damp places, dressed like the poor relations of Merlin, himself undone by Bugs Bunny, the wily rabbit.

And so the children — behind a mask they think their real identities are concealed — saw fit to offer the world of adults a choice of trick or treat. And why not? Is generosity a fault? It was a time to scare the tall ones, to put matches under their feet, and powder puffs on their seats, soap their mothers' garters, and stick tongues out and laugh and mimic adult inanities. A boy dressed as a pope went about blessing dead leaves. Some children thought it was the secret of the magic of the masks that protected them. Others felt there must have been one of those conventions, that at once scared and delighted the children, which was itself a mystery, where the adults had met to decide to become helpless to attack and beat them. It was the time of freedom; short, intense; a few evening hours of song and laughter and jubilation.

It was no doubt at one of those many conventions of adults from which children are banned that it was also decided to subvert the holiday. They, the tall ones, readily proved amongst themselves that in reality this merriment was not the fault of all the children but merely of some distinctly malcontent and tiny fringe minority composed of those who would probably grow up lunatic anyway. In any case, the holiday, it was shown, was of necessity insidious, and possibly under the domination of a foreign ideology. The very tone of their laughter gave them all away. They introduced the Sandman, come to put you to sleep.

The leading edge of the subversion was to convince the kids that if adults offered a treat the proper rules of conduct forbade a trick. For emphasis it was made plain that violators would be caught and beaten. The adults meanwhile had privately decided to blow their minds with sugar.

And so it came to pass once again that pleasure was banned from the world. The feast of sugar freaks is now composed of little bumpkins in uniforms purchased at the corner drugstore and the five-and-dime; with these they come with shopping bags and beg for candy— of lollipops and candy bars, of chocolate drops and sugar plums and dandy coated apples; later they gather in clumps to compare their hauls, the mothers overseeing and clapping.

Certain passions seek their excesses. It is so with the hatred for children. It begins early. At birth they are held upside down and slapped until they scream. The first experience of the world is terror. It goes on. Who has not known of children stuffed in boxes, brought up in closets? who has not seen images of their bodies, broken of arm and rib, stained and bruised, with cigarette burns, emaciated so much it seems they'll snap, and bulging haunted eyes in living rooms across the country, like the eyes on the victims of the concentration camps? So now for holloween — eve celebrating the hollow victory over children — cookies are prepared with cyanide and razor blades, and candycane sprinkled with arsenic, and candy bars with toothpick ends and broken glass. It seems, for some at any rate, to pass the time of day.

The Trial

"I had a dream," Tom says, passing his hand over his eyes. "We had taken a low road in the hills beyond Anapaest and come to a bog with only a dry strip of land across it." It grew dark and began to rain, a hard pelting rain, driving at them almost on the horizontal and they had to get down on their hands and knees and dig their fingers into the path to avoid being flushed into the bog.

They were heading toward a building they couldn't see but they knew was there, as surely as they would in a dream have such certainty; it lay beyond the bog, a big administration building in pseudogothic, with plaques on either side of the main entrance, full of curses and exhortations, and two statues, one of a woman without eyes who held an apothecary's scale, and the other, of an old man, leaning on a scythe.

And still they made their way, blinking the rain out of their eyes, when he — Tom — saw the train materialize as it were, on the left out of the rain and fog, sleek and greyish black, an old steam engine, with only a piece of the tender visible behind it. It fumed and clunked, its giant black metal wheels poised and still. It seemed so warm, somehow alive, watching them. And Slim was holding Tom's wrist, whispering, no, no, it's not for us...

Beyond the bog they were under arrest and walked with their hands manacled behind their backs, guarded by men with iron faces and jack boots. They were taken to the administrative building, cold like a morgue, with the sick smell of formaldehyde and ether in the halls. It made Tom sick and cold and full of fear.

In the trial room there was a judge with the look, the smug look, characteristic of a frightening and impenetrable stupidity. And Tom trembled. He tried to hide his eyes so they would not see his panic. There is no way out. There is the noise of the placing of thick metal bars over the windows and the drawing of the blinds. The audience is full of cripples, all kinds of people deformed and drooling and sticky. They are just ordinary people who have been turned inside out.

The judge says, the accused will stand. The clerk will read the charges. And the clerk says, Your Honor, they are accused of— Of what? of what? Tom thinks, frantic; it sounded like voomvoom. How do you plead? the judge asks.

I do not plead, Tom says and Slim says, I do not plead. The judge says, so be it. The clerk will enter the plea, no contest. Will the prosecution state its case? We shall, Your Honor, they were brought here. It is clear that they are guilty, Your Honor, in every way most culpable. So be it, the judge says.

You have been found guilty of the foulest of crimes. If you were a little younger you might hope to be called little naughty bastards. But I will tell you, we do not try children here, only criminals. You cannot oppose us forever and think to get away with it. You are fools to think otherwise. I trust you realize the political crime is the only kind of crime against which, and for the moment, all manner of torture is permissible. But even if you don't so realize, it doesn't matter, for ignorance of the law is no bargain.

Still, in pronouncing sentence upon you, I shall be lenient, I shall be kind. I would not be, of my own volition, more pernicious than the law.

You are to be taken to the place of sacrifice, there to have your eyes plucked out with the plucking spoon. Then you shall be set out upon the desert, to wander till death claims your miserable carcasses. So it is said and so it shall be carried out, as mercy commands it.

"That's about the way it went," says Slim, "except the end. We are to be turned over to psychosurgeons for corrective surgery."

Tom's eyes blink several times.

"You have been in a daze for a long time," Slim says, so relieved now to see Tom again, he forgets everything and leans forward from the position he was in, sitting on his heels, and wraps his arms around his friend. They remain so a long time, huddled together in the darkness.

They are in a cell. On the ceiling is a 40 watt bulb in a wire cage. The walls are stone, black with the body oils of prisoners who passed here and scratched their anguish. There are no marks on the stone, no words for those who come after, no defiance, the oils only, black and rancid, of those who waited to die.

Tom shakes his head to clear the cobwebs from his mind.

"We are accused of many things," Slim says.

The lousy books they read corrupted a pair of decent electricians. What are you now? the prosecutor shouted. One — pointing the finger at Tom — a sleazy intellectual, the other his sidekick. One — pointing the finger at Slim — a rough and tumble master, the other his acolyte. Shaven yes, but unkempt. How do they make a living? Their papers say they are at present clowns on unemployment. I ask you, is that credible? Your Honor, I submit that thinking distorts the soul and makes of honest working men subversive wags, the playthings of those who would destroy us and take our coonskins off the wall. They have abused of our patience. For that, Your Honor, I pledge their deaths! I eat their ears! Who — I ask — who has given them permission to feel? And why — if they must think — can't they think like everybody else? Because they have been perverted. We shall leave that to the psychosurgeons and behaviorists to correct. I do not presume, myself, to be an expert in the field.

But I ask you, was there no religion to suit their tastes? Could they not afford to yield inwardly a little? Or practice some deceit? like Shakespeare said?

Cut off their balls! somebody roared.

Make them eat spoons!

The cripples in the audience howled and smeared each other with their blood and threw little blessed plastic bags of it at the judge and the prosecution, weeping the while and gnawing on their fingers, having orgasms at the touch of chairs and walls and little Christmas ornaments that some, by subterfuge, had snuck into the court, expecting here today a mass orgasm like the last spasm of the dying, so dear to the heart of the executioner. They cut and stabbed each other and howled and rolled their heads from side to side in ecstasy. The judge meanwhile had gotten to his feet and laid his penis on the bench and stood there pounding it with the gavel. The prosecuting attorneys tore out their hair and poked out their eyes, laughing hysterically...

The cell is still. They see the sallow of their own faces, dimly in the light.

"This isn't sadness, Tom."

"No— I know."

The walls are hard and real. The stone is cold. It is the place of death. It is its way to come like this, suddenly, without warning.

They turn sharply to the sound from down the hall of a bolt slammed back and a door bursting open. The wall, though it is there, seems to dissolve as does the one beyond and the one beyond. They can see the lone and solitary naked bodies in the adjoining cells of a woman and a child and a man.

The jailers rush into the farthest cell, armed with truncheon and blackjack, lead pipe and baseball bat. Their eyes are wild, their brains boil, their lips are thick with spit. They are naked, genitals erect, circling like dogs about to take on their wounded prey for the last time. And yet they hang there, weapons raised, as though the ultimate satisfaction would be to see the inner terror of the victim break all resistance, the very physiological thread of life, and the victim die.

But the man, the victim, does not die. The helplessness and terror are not enough. They fall on him and beat him hard, and their rage rises with each blow and groan until he lies a bloody twitching lump of flesh.

They stop then, and one nudges him with his foot and spits on the body. They breathe hard, they sweat. It means nothing to them for a victim to be helpless without knowing it. His unconsciousness robs them of his humiliation.

It is at this moment, frequently, that out of disgust the victim is killed. What good is he?

They rush out. And once again a bolt slams back and a door bursts open— into the next cell. On hands and knees, naked, as they, she turns to face her executioners. She has a spasm, a bowl full of vomit gushes out.

Tom and Slim look away from the naked figure crouching on the floor. They fix their sight on each other's eyes; these flinch, pain and fear creep into them. There is a little silence before another bolt slams nearer and more loud, and another door bursts back into the cell of the child next door. They had seen a pair of great sad eyes. In all the time there is only a small cry from him, like a quick whine.

Slowly they rise, with the sounds of breaking bones in their ears, and face the door.

The bolt is drawn with the same slam.

He stands framed in the doorway, a common man in a black suit and white shirt collar. His hair is black. There is no white to his eyes. A dog sits beside him, with short, pointed ears and lips that do not cover his teeth; his eyes are also without whites; his tail curls a half a dozen times around his paws. His name is Onetwo; with his tail he lassos victims and with his teeth he tears out their eyes and then he sets the blind loose.

"My name is Alexander Puke," the man says. He points a palm at Tom and Slim: "don't speak."

They couldn't anyway. They are paralyzed, complete with the terror that comes in dreams when one tries to flee, compulsive and futile gesture. The air chokes in the throat, cutting off screams; the body thrashes; they know the foreboding of exhaustion and helplessness.

His voice is a sound of gravel moving over gravel. "I am the only one you have to fear."

Why then do they feel so strongly that he lies?

The right eye begins to move — socket, orb and lid and brow descending together to stop in the middle of the cheek — blinking; and both ears turn to face forward.

Dizzy, nauseous, their ears ring, eyesight blurs. Their throats, bringing a burning bitter taste of bile, begin to make the sounds of bodies caught in the dry heaves.

And then Slim screams, a combination of anguish and rebellion:

"All right! be done with it!"

Puke cocks his head and looks at them, almost as though he were perplexed; then he kicks the dog and moves aside and with a small wave of the hand that gives them permission, says with total calm, "you may go."

Their feet are free to move. The dry heaves stop. Their bodies are abruptly cool inside clothes drenched in sweat. They walk in single file into the hall and turn. A long and narrow stairway leads upward into a ring of light.

It seems they walk and walk and never once look back although they sense the building, the same, in pseudogothic, with donjon and ancient battlements that are nor real, possessed of high and narrow windows, looking after them, immobile as it is, like the train.

It takes forever for it to disappear from mind.

They sit silently on a knoll in the soft grass and watch their legs tremble. There is no shame to fear. And afterwards they crawl over to the oak and rest their heads against it, curled up on their sides in fetal silence and fall asleep. It is a long and dreamless sleep. The wind comes and gently moves the grass and leaves and moves their hair.

Tom awakens first and rises and walks a few steps away to turn and take in the morning. Ever since somebody said there will come a time when the morning will not come again, he seems to enjoy it more, from an awareness perhaps that it too is transient. Slim has propped himself up on one elbow.

Tom looks back to the mountains far behind them, shrouded in an orographic rain. Ahead of them lie broken hills. They will take the road in a little while— to where? To other cellars? It seems all to little purpose.

"It will be a hot day," he says.

Slim remains motionless.

The image of the prison rises between them, blurred, strained with fear, like the concentration camps of their own world. They remember together without saying so the prisons inside the camps, and instruments of torture inside the prisons. When death is all around do people cease to think of it? They grit their teeth, dominated, some say, by the will to survive. But survival was never everything. It does not account for the woman who gave her rations to a child that was not hers, who might not itself even survive, accepting thus for herself disease, even death. The war ended before she could die. After, in her house, she hid little stocks of food for herself, from her family; they pretended they did not see her rise every night, for months, to consume morsels of what she had hidden. It does not account for those who broke into the camps to organize resistance. Organize resistance...

Tom is pensive. "There never was a paradise to regain," he says, "a lost innocence. There was only one to make—"

"And?"

"And look at this." Tom makes a circular gesture, to mean this place, this time. "It seems as though they are as far away from it as we ever have been."

Slim sits up. "You could say we've always been chasing rainbows."

"There's worse," Tom says. "What if the moment came—and we missed it."

Yes, what if. What if the opportunity had been on a train going to North Carolina and everyone was looking in the direction of Minnesota? It would be too late now, wouldn't it.

Slim gets to his feet. Enough of this. It's like living in a cellar full of anguish. The valleys to the east are bathed in sunlight. Slim motions silently toward them and they walk. They do not speak. They have lost their hats. The lilies are open among the pads on a pond. At 2,000 feet hawks watch for rabbits. He thinks, you cannot cup the world in your hand. Which is like saying you cannot know its possibilities.

What is certain is we grow old, we get tired, we die. Others come to hope...

What does it matter that everything tends inexorably toward the long oblivion? Hominids roamed the Earth millions of years back. Man himself may have been around a couple of million years. There is a life span of species—? So be it. It is queer that accidents on distant stars may alter life here— but why not?

Those who make a point of calculating these things say the day will come when the stars will wink out. We will be left looking across a gaseous cloud from our position on a spiral arm toward the center of the galaxy. They say there is no night there, so dense are the stars. They say the sun will grow old and large, and turn the Earth into a land of fire, until the sun cools and turns the Earth to ice; they say the star may go supernova and the globe we are on will be consumed in the apocalypse; or yet the sun may implode, as it were, become a black hole sucking our speck of cosmic dust and all passing light into it and eternal obscurity. They say, what of the dark companion to our sun? And what of centripetal force that might yet affect a reversal of direction in the universe? They speak of muons and quarks and charms— They also say there is no room to complain, and no need; by then, by the time of any of these events, the species will have long disappeared. When I am dead, someone said, the universe will have died but just for me— and you and I will have ceased to sing and birds my mother knitted on my sweaters will have fallen away from flight—

The day to day destruction of man and mountain and ant and flower is for some a kind of dress rehearsal for the final thing; others project a cosmic destiny in the vision of the species leaving this place to populate the stars, its only link to Earth a memory.

Around the here and now the darkness gathers. Yet it is not possible that the man was right who said we yearn for the silence of the womb (whether or not he knew it is not silent), as though life were some force wretched out of death, to which we yearn to return. The Ibo goddess of the underworld receives the dead into her womb. But the Greeks drew the name of the abode of the gods at Delphi from the word delphi, the uterus. Old myths are not ancient wisdom lost. They are ancient hopes, acclimatizations, adjustments, the spirit that overcomes a closed destiny of pain and horror and death.

The Circus Tender

They are surprised to round a bend and see a city of tents and painted wagons. There are pennants and miles of rope, and pegs, and sawdust; complete with the odor of horse manure and cow dung and stale laughter. The carousel is still, so are all the music boxes. It's the time of day when the circus rests.

"I understand you're a couple of electricians."

It is with this that they meet Harvey Miracle Onedime, who has come up from behind. The Grey Corpulence he is called behind his back (he weighs 350 pounds). His belly starts below his chin and ends just above his knees. It creates an optical illusion when facing him: he seems to be leaning back and looking down his nose. He has two eyes like a common man. He wears a foot wide necktie and a pinstriped suit. He is the circus tender, master of the tents, lord of the rings. He smiles with one side of his face only. The other side evaluates the sucker.

We're not electricians," Slim says.

"Oh?" Onedime hates to be misinformed.

"We were clowns. I was the roustabout. Tom here was the clown who plays with the light."

"If you can breathe, I can use you. Clowns is good. I don't pay union wages."

Which means, simply, you're hired.

"Get your act together. You go on tonight."

Onedime avoids looking at the sampan in the canal. He has a memory of the time he had come up like this, immaculate and dignified, and once finished with the business at hand, had made the grand gesture of departure to blow the sucker's mind by stepping off onto his private sampan and floating off with a couple of broads dressed in neckties fanning him. The sampan broke and sank. He had put a good face on this mortification, smiling as he brushed the canal mud away and picked a little wriggling fish out of his ear. Later the sampan dealer and the two broads were found in the canal with anchors around their necks. The sucker was blown apart in the fun house.

"We're travelling east," says Tom.

"So is the circus," Onedime says. "You're looking for a clear passage? You got it. The word has been moving east ahead of you that you are a couple of troublemakers. I'm not worried."

Why should he be? He seems ageless, powerful, lords it from the top of the heap. He walks around with a couple of politicians in his pockets, he buys and sells legal battles, the Crime Syndicate owes him a few favors; he is rumored to make a meal from a ten pound steak and a gallon of German beer every night in the company of assorted members of the high and mighty.

"I can be friendly," he says. "Try me."

With that he boards his private car on the kiddie train and is pulled away, like James Joyce would say, chug-chug.

The circus guards walk around with mastiffs and Doberman pinschers with snouts in wire cages, guarding peace and order. They tip their hats to Tom and Slim, the others growl.

Tom's act, in center ring, follows that of a juggler who juggles six bowling pins and a coffin. The supreme moment comes when the juggler captures the pins, dives into the coffin while it is in midair, the lid snaps shut, the coffin falls and hits the ground and disappears. By comparison Houdini was a mere lock picker.

Tom's face under the tophat is chalk white, with the mascara of burnt sienna outlining a pronounced droop to the eyes and mouth. He has a broom and with it he sweeps together into one a half dozen spots from the klieg lights, then sweeps around the edges of the single spot until it is no bigger than the palm of the hand. He sweeps it up into his palm and brings it closer to his face and studies it from above and from the side and at the oblique until, with a great shrug, places it in his pocket and the light dies.

There has always been at this moment, and there is now, a murmur in the crowd, like a ripple of surprise from this dying, and a cool dampness whisked in by a giant silent fan above. It is — who needs to say it? — like a visitation. It has happened that children cry at the sudden dying of the light. Others turn to moaning and gnashing of the teeth.

It seems to be a long time before the single spot emerges from his pocket, on his palm, like a candle in the penumbra. He is on his knees. His head is cocked. He puts the light down gently so it will not break, and with his fingers he pushes from the center out. The light resists, shrinks and expands and then expands for good under his patient hands. Out of the shadows of the center ring emerge the jugglers and clowns, the aerialists and acrobats and animal tamers with their cats and elephants and bears and dogs. They have gathered to watch the birth of light. Tom's face changes out of sadness as he works. Judging the spot large enough, he stands and pulls a handful of powder from his pocket that mushrooms like a puffball when he throws it on the spot and the light explodes. It rains spots of light that grow and grow until they merge and it becomes as bright as day inside the tent. By then he wears the smile of victory. The music blares. The animals roar. The happy clown, his hat off, his hair wild, tumbles his way out.

"Mine," says Harvey, sweeping his hand over the throng and tents. There are people enough for every game and every show. "Stick with me, boys. I'll make you rich."

He fishes a metal box out of his pocket and opens it. "Candied lice," he says, "a delicacy. Have one."

They refuse. He scowls.

"Ah—" he says, "I liked Tom's act. It was meaningless, the best kind. It put me in an expansive mood. —Do you know what I deplore?"

They are walking past the shooting gallery where a mouse runs desperately back and forth. Tom and Slim are dressed again in clean spats and tails and hats.

"I deplore the passing of the automobile. It was the perfect product. Absolutely perfect."

A trace of skepticism crosses the faces of Tom and Slim.

"Look," Onedime says, "I'm willing to take a little more from you because you're a couple of clowns, but it would be better if you remembered the world isn't a stage. I like a little awe around me when I talk. Understood?"

"Understood."

"Good. So listen, learn something. Don't be a pair of assholes all your lives."

They tip their hats to him.

"All right," says Onedime, satisfied. He passes a hand over his face to remove the smirk and put it in his pocket, such is the depth of his frugality.

"When you think of the car," he says, "what comes to your mind? that it killed more people than all the wars of all the people put together?"

This argument was done to death in other days, to convey perhaps the equality of the dead, so why complain?

"Sometimes," says Slim, "I think of the lead that filled the air. Other times, I remember the Earth was raped to build it—"

Onedime laughs. "You can't rape an old whore, my little chum."

"It was inefficient," says Tom, casting about for an argument that might impress the practical man.

Again Onedime laughs. The thought patterns of nincompoops are a source of ceaseless amusement to him.

"Try to realize," he says, "the train and bicycle, in tandem, could move a hundred percent more people into every nook and cranny at six or seven times the speed, in nearly complete safety for a fraction of the cost. The car was, for the purpose for which it was built — to move people around — the most inefficient thing ever devised.

"That was, my little friends, its grace, its beauty, the stroke of genius. No one could have accomplished that. It needed a climate in which to thrive, an understanding of time, motion, and freedom that was nothing short of delirious. I know these things are hard for the common man to understand. Let me explain.

"It goes like this. The major problem of making profit is that the objects you sell stick around. Ideally, they should evaporate with the completion of the sale. Concretely, how long they last is how long they cut into your profit. Even cardboard houses last 40 or 50 years."

They pass the Hall of Mirrors, the bingo tables, the spun sugar on a paper cone. Some children are on leashes. Others are made to give a paw and say hello to the nice gentleman. A little further on, in the privacy of a corner, a lady is pissing in her hat.

"You never saw cars clutter highways," says Tom.

"Who has?" Harvey retorts. "It must have been a marvel to behold— like an insanity without purpose."

A flock of peace doves have been trained to hover a few feet above his head. Occasionally he reaches up and pulls one down. The bird, in fright, shits out its brains. He bites its head off with his teeth and plucks it while it bleeds. That done he pops it in his mouth and chomps down a dozen times or so before he swallows it.

"Now then," he says, smacking his lips, "to make a profit you have to produce. So. Suppose you want to go like hell, produce furiously, and get nowhere, so you could keep going like hell— suppose that, my little friends, admittedly an ideal situation. Well, the car did it.

"It consumed hundreds of millions of manhours, literally ate raw materials, crippled and decimated millions, made possible the spread of the cities into endless suburbs, demanded miles and miles of roads that trucks could use nearly for free (that cut the throat of the railroads by the way; which was convenient since the problem of destroying them had become a real stickler). The car substituted the inefficient for the efficient, the costly for the cheap, and in less than 10 years it was ready for the garbage dump. Requiring what, my little friends? What? Ceaseless renewal. Like producing paper to burn it. In the cycle of the average's man life he could burn five to seven cars! Is that beautiful?"

He has paused at a drinking fountain to wash the blood of the dove from his fingers. He whips out a towelette from an inside breast pocket and pats his fingers dry, wiping carefully around the giant ring on his right hand (it bears, in stone, a carving of his mother).

"You would think the car could do no more. You're wrong. Naturally. Its ultimate glory was to bring a measure of social peace to the human rabblement. I know, I know, it puzzles you. I'll explain.

"Imagine, for a moment, if a lot of people wanted to get together for a meeting, like people used to do in the cities at the drop of a stupid hat, jump down into the streets— a hundred, two hundred thousand, a half a million would swarm in no time. In the suburbs, they'd have to drive someplace, probably to a giant parking lot, and create a monumental traffic jam to get there; most of them would never get there. Just the idea of it turned them off; they'd think of sitting there, bumper to bumper, breathing exhaust fumes; they had enough of that going to work and coming back.

"For hundreds — what am I saying? — for thousands of years we worried about mobs, and plotted how to quiet them, and here, at a stroke, and passively, the car removed the problem. To make a problem vanish, *that* is a true mark of progress, the unmistakable imprint of high civilization."

He pats his flanks with pudgy hands and looks around, approving and content, curling his lower lip outward.

"But," he says, "the car is gone. I have no real regrets. Live with your time, I say. That's what it means to be a man. Ah my little friends," — he spreads his arms wide — "you clowns, this is the midway, the Walk of Light, the citadel of civilization, at once its museum and highest expression."

The motto of the circus is, Where Onedime Is There Is No Night. The world is flooded by artificial light.

They pass a doctor in a cage. He is on a leash. He is, so Harvey says, a recalcitrant and so will be in the natural course of events, a demonstration model for a lobotomy when we get around to it. He used to be young and now he is old. Beyond, there is the room of Professor Moriarty, the fiend of crime, empty as always (the word is, through Sherlock Holmes, that he is dead but in this matter the word of Mr. Holmes has been shown to err). On the left is Chicamauga Patsy, the stone maker. She is chained to a wall so she will not move. She can only be viewed indirectly as a reflection in a mirror, for her nipples are little fingers that beckon men to their doom.

On the right, in a glass cage like the others, stands a giant of a man. The legend on the plaque says, he is nearly eight feet tall, nearly 800 pounds; a mountain of a man with wild and matted hair, a burly hairy man with nails like claws (for two reasons this: one, he has put in no requisition for nail clippers, and two, being in the nude, he has no pockets where he could keep them). His name is Ferdinand de Carnivore, formerly Billy Blunderpickle. The legend says he was found in the hills of Arkansas. He clutches half chewed babies in either paw.

Tom and Slim have fallen back; they turned pale.

Onedime laughs. "You think it is barbaric. Good, good. But it's an illusion, my little friends, like your baloney with the light. Our high civilization would not condone it. I myself would not tolerate it.

"You don't see what you see there, because you think you see children but those," — he points triumphant — "those are merely laboratory products, test-tube babies."

The giant drools blood, crushing the bloody masses in his hands against the glass.

Slim leans on the iron picket fence. Tom looks to his friend. But as one man they force themselves to look on the giant and then turn to face Onedime. There are limits.

"I grant," — Harvey Miracles is vexed — "that you are a couple of kooks. But surely you recognize the marvel of science that has made of cannibalism a diversion, a pastime, a mere sideshow? Think of the advances in science manifested here, the gain in sophistication."

Their disgust upsets him. Is not our control over the genetic code a triumph?

"You scoff?" he says, not a question, it's an accusation.

"It's good to scoff, it clears the throat." This from Slim.

"What are you— one of these sleazy malcontents?"

Slim shakes his head. "I am really a gentle man with a kind and unforgiving heart."

Onedime only seems to ignore the remark. He presses his cufflinks against his arms, he looks around, he licks his lips, he curls the lower one outward and shakes his head.

"Okay, okay. Let's get off this track."

He points to various notables in the crowd— there is Jacques de la Couillonerie, the famous French theologian. And there! the tall gentleman with the gray sideburns and the gloves of a funeral director. It is Felix von Graft. Felix is dressed in a black suit, vest, white shirt and tie, derby. The suit comes with two pairs of pants; the second pair is rolled into a bag on his back, giving him a hunched look. A man of verve and quick wits, he was launched on a brilliant career as a salesman of used faucet washers when he was spotted by General Glozover Pangrave. The general hired him to lobby for new weapons. The campaign slogan was, Grenades Are Nicer Ear Rings, and A Rifle in Every Closet. He was given a test to see if he could recognize on which side butter was spread on a piece of bread. Now an elder statesman, he wears the highest title, defender of the faith and experimental apologist.

And there! Above the crowd, are the head and shoulders of a man, in profile, moving without bounce. Patrick Makepiece Warmonger, shrewd, calculating, a brain like a filing cabinet, a Secretary of State to end all secretaries of state, a master of transparent circumspection. As he passes through a hole in the crowd it is seen that six boys in harnesses pull a flat cart. On the flat cart a chair is affixed, encrusted with gold and men in war chariots brandishing spears. And on the chair Warmonger sits, a tub of lard with hands folded across his middle parts. His eyes are large, exorbited, rheumy; the bottom of his jowls rests on his shoulders; his chins roll over his chest, his gut rolls over his knees, but he is serene; they say he thinks.

Two others have joined the party. Onedime introduces them as friends of the circus. The first he calls Sir Arthur Clarendon Mountbank, and the other, Hans Furst von First und Last. One is as thin as a rail, the other sports a monocle; both wear raincoats and derbies and pinstriped trousers.

"Vhat ist loose here?" says Hans, which is German for the question, what is going on? "Durink a var vunce men strained de feces of udder men for undigested grain, vould jew prefer ve make a scene of zat?"

"I have often wondered, Hans," says Sir Arthur Mountbank, "why you simply must affect a speech impediment. It is rather unbecoming."

"Ach! Swine!" says von Last, slapping himself on the forehead. "I forgot." He bows to Tom and Slim, without lifting his eyes from them. "We was over there drinking firewater, Mountbank and I. It spun my brain. My apologies."

"Well, I leave you to my colleagues," Onedime says. "I'm off to the exhibition."

The rumor is that by this expression he means he likes to undress before a captive audience of little children. It is also said he enters a closet to play with the bones of his dead mother. After which he will take a bubble bath in a concoction composed of four carcinogens and bicarbonate of soda. And so he goes, his birds aflutter around him.

"A queer fellow, our dear Onedime," Sir Arthur muses. "He has, you know, obscene sexual desires."

He shrugs, and pauses for a moment to study the giant Ferdinand, urinating against the glass.

"I dream of mutilation," says Mountbank, "like other men dream of caresses. A pretty scene, this. (He means Ferdinand.) Trite but pretty. Too much gore, too little pain. —Shall we go, gentlemen?"

"Go?" Slim asks. He does not sound accommodating.

"Mr. Onedime's instructions are to show you around. You can see anything you wish. Then we are to dispose of you. — Tut-tut," Sir Arthur admonishes, "I would not look for an exit, gentlemen. Hans is fully armed."

"Dis ist de truce," agrees von Last.

"By the king's urine, Hans!"

"Ach!" — again he slaps his head and pops the monocle — "swine heart! dumb cop! I forgot."

"I must say, it's an exasperating habit, my good fellow."

"Furst," says Tom, "doesn't that mean prince?"

"Gestalt, Mein Herr! Sprechen Sie Deutsch?"

"Nine."

The eyes of First und Last nearly drop out of his head they are so downcast.

So Slim decides to cheer him up. "What kind of weapon do you have?"

"A 9-mm Walther with silencer. I have two of them. I have razor blades in the heel of one shoe. I have cyanide pellets imbedded in bubblegum. I have two fragmentation grenades, one smoke grenade. Back in the tent I have a 28-mm SpzB, a 75-mm recoilless rifle, an 88-mm Panzerkanone, 150-mm Nebelwerfer, a .22 caliber high velocity fire—"

Mountbank holds up both hands. "By the king's feces, you have found his weakness! Myself I prefer to wire clients to a variable intensity transformer. Shall we go on?"

He has that gesture of the hand, ineffable combination of politeness and disdain, that marks a man of good breeding.

"We have until dawn, I presume?" asks Tom.

"Till dawn, of course, " replies Sir Arthur.

They are introduced in passing to one of von Last's favorite guards, Euglena Escariot who guides two giant dogs, Hansel and Gretel. In the pursuit of a routine tonsillectomy, the surgeon mistook the larynx of Euglena for his tonsils. Undaunted, the Euglena increased his efficiency a thousand fold by proceeding directly to the action, bypassing the business of questioning. Where there's a will there's a way. Certainly his life exemplifies that.

In the House of Fairy Tales the fat lady sits trapped in a tub while her back L'il Peter Pumpkin scrubs. He is dressed in a loincloth with an empty quiver of arrows on his back and thirteen custard pies stacked one on the other. In the corner Mother Goose grossly rhymes, effectively senile. The air is filled in *contravoce* with the music of Joe-Ann C.-Bastion Batch. Next door, in the Canvas House, people are bowled over by a giant rubber ball. They hear its whoosh and whack. The walls are curved and slick. The people are nude and greased. There is no way out. The fun lasts half an hour. As always here, in the excitement, Hans wets his pants and has to be taken to the little boys' room.

On the way out of there, Tom says, "Abraham Lincoln said, 'those who deny freedom to others deserve it not for themselves.' Well, he had suspended the writ of habeas corpus so people could be arbitrarily arrested, but it was adjudicated after the fact and decided he did not have the right to suspend the right of people to have a corpse so *he* was arrested and thrown into solitary confinement and forgotten for a while. Later on somebody happened to open the door and they found this fellow there who had shrunk two inches and claimed to be Lincoln. They threw *him* into the bughouse where he spent his time walking up and down saying, I am Lincoln and they would say to him if you are Lincoln why aren't you two inches taller? How could he answer this? He never got out. It is said he is the grandfather of all those Lincolns, long and short, bald and hairy, who to this day claim they are Lincoln. Now," — he raises a finger — "now the enigma is, how can one (you or I, say) not be Lincoln and believe it?"

As it happens, enigmas are painful to von Last. Accordingly they go with this one to the gazer into crystal balls, Cassandra Figitit, called by her friends Pussy Cocoa. They look around and call and look around. But they do not find her. She is hiding under the covers chewing on her toenails, terrified by what she saw earlier in her ball, a worm chewing on her eye.

Once on the outside Tom holds up a finger and says, "There was a cry heard a long time ago on the night train to Toledo: the rhododendrons are coming, it said, the rhododendrons are coming! Unfortunately the cry was not heeded, whence the common saying, the people have become vegetables."

Hans von Last stands trembling, petrified, eyes flicking left and right, his mind consumed with the thought of being eaten alive by a vegetable.

"He cannot tolerate these bloody enigmas," Mountbank cries. "Desist or I shall be forced to slay you forthwith by my own hand."

"Did you know," says Tom to him, "that in Chicago it is unlawful to experience erection in a public place?"

Mountbank pales, making then and there, to himself, the secret promise never to go to Chicago.

And then all fall silent for they have entered Science House. It is a tall and luminous place, with a passageway between speakers and exhibitions.

The tent is gray and rippled, made to look like an interior view of the lobes and convolutions of the brain. All the exhibitions and their speakers are in boxes, each box and site and voice are the engrams of the brain. Here then, assembled in a waterproof environment, is the ultimate in man's development.

Tom and Slim turn immediately to the left toward the less well lit places of dusty unpacked crates and empty sandwich bags and used condoms. A rat scurries. A spider has flies tangled in its web but sits in the corner, contemplating what? Somebody hits a trip wire or they pass through an activator beam — someone has closed a synaptic circuit — and a voice says, like a lament, on a morose baritone, "Science serves, you say."

They stop.

The voice raises little puffs of dust out of the speakers.

"That's not enough, not nearly enough. Which one of us suppressed the word that makes all the difference: science serves what? The word, like a pandora box, releases a bunch of others— serves to what end? and from what purpose? and in what direction? Science does not seek in any direction, at random, detached. It does not even seek in those directions that present themselves to the conception. It looks where it is told, or thinks it is told, or where the money tells it to look. And the spirit of it is known by its direction.

"What do you remember of the routine mutilation of animals? —how it began with rats and mice and spread toward the dog, the monkey, the man. It is a science of cages and constraint and burns and drugs. It moves from mutilation to mutilation.

"We should be pleased with the discoveries of biochemistry, with star travel, with the penetration of the ocean depths, yet these things are mostly cause for fear. Let me remind you of human specimens given terminal diseases, or those who have been put in ice boxes so others may study the effects and see how long they will take to freeze. The ultimate good of the species is the crime that justifies all the others. They have been distorted who now preside over a world of pain and grief, horror and death. They no longer even recognize it for what it is. You are in the hands of torturers with good intentions. Beware of those who believe in mutilation and death, beware," — the record or tape or whatever it is that generates the power of speech in this engram crackles — "beware... I say—"

A guard appears, a figure with disc shaped eyes and pale immobile flesh over bone; a synthetic white blood corpuscle? He wears white gloves. "Regrettably, gentlemen, the suppression of this engram has not, so far, been successful. It is admittedly, like a bad dream. Meanwhile—" He makes a slow sweeping gesture with one arm, keeping the elbow close to the body, "go forth! go forth and marvel!"

They return to the light. It is fluorescent and slightly bluish, like sight through a bruised eye. The crates are stacked and open on one side, allowing a vision of what lies within. There. A group of physicists hold hands and dance round a mushroom cloud. Its residue, a pile of corpses, lies in a far corner. A voice in overlay offers a quiet disquisition on the benefits of overkill, a kind of democratic euthanasia. In a smaller box to one side an aged physicist discourses at length on his regrets. When he gets to a particularly long and tedious point, he says blah-blah-blah and so forth, in a soft low voice, to represent his anguish, and then resumes. Another, above him, speaks of the nuclear mining of Mars, the ancient abode of the god of war.

On the right they are germinating Ferdinand's dinner. And a guard makes his way up the dizzying pile of boxes to reach on the topmost one a wary vulture that somehow got in here, probably without a ticket.

Three geneticists stand like proud fathers looking over a tomato with the head of a frog: a hybrid, naturally, to allow the tomato to better defend itself against insects. The three are prepared to share the honors. Meanwhile, behind the boxes, two scientists with cudgels beat each others' brains out, in fearful determined silence; above them waits a little prize for the winner, by a former manufacturer of dynamite. Tom and Slim go take a peek, with Hans close behind them. Again a guard guides them back, explaining that what is critical is what's up front. Man is a beast of conflict, we all know that?

They find Clarendon Mountbank watching a man in a box in a maze getting little shocks with every wrong turn; he does not know there are no correct turns and that the object of the experiment is to see which goal he reaches first, apathy or insanity. It is a critical social experiment. Tom thinks he recognizes in the victim a man he had seen earlier, riding on the carousel.

Sir Arthur signals to the others. "Interesting," he says, visibly excited, "look at the expression on the faces of the experimenters. They do not even seem to enjoy it."

"Robots?" suggests von Last.

"Unlikely, my good fellow. It is far simpler to truncate the emotive structure of an individual than to create a robot with this diversity of function. Furthermore, these can be taught to copulate and reproduce their kind. A robot system would require a vast and possibly prohibitive capital outlay. Remarkable," he concludes, "remarkable."

He turns to Hans. "It is an indication, my dear von Last, that our days are numbered."

Hans smiles only. He has other convictions.

"It stinks of death in here," Slim says, and waves his arm, and nearly knocks over a boxful of scientists who have all fallen into a corner and cringe before the unforeseeable gestures of this giant beast outside their box.

Tom and Slim have had enough, glimpsing only out of the corners of their eyes as they streak toward the exit at the other end, a laser beam, a lightning bolt, a mouth open with all the teeth showing, a cloud of civilians reduced to twitching and imbecility (a new military weapon that keeps the bodies functional for the mines).

Beyond the exit, Friedrich von Nacht and Nabel, the eminent psychiatrist, sits. They call him Uncle. He plays with a swigglestick in a puddle of muddy water. He looks up as they come.

"When is the last time you had a change in dreams?" he asks, a baritone full of professional concern.

But they rush on.

"Come and see me," he yells after them, "come and see me soon. I can correct your errors, make you accept and live peacefully with your unseemly side."

He gets to his feet and raises his voice a notch, shaking his fist, "Don't forget, you too are a horror on the inside!"

Too late. They're already out of earshot. He mumbles to himself, "Bastards! Ingrates!" and returns to the swigglestick in the mud.

It is coming dawn.

"Shall we retire to my tent?" Sir Arthur asks.

They turn off the main drag into the alleyways where the tents are not so smart, their ropes are slack, they lack upkeep, lean dogs look for bones. There are muddy paths everywhere with boards thrown at random across them. The air is permeated with the smell of urine.

Von Last has cocked his derby forward and to one side. His hands are thrust into the pockets of his jacket where he taps into the power of the 9-mm Walther.

"My abode," says Mountbank at the entrance to a tent. One side is flanked by a potted plant, the other by a small gallows. Mountbank removes a glove to touch a leaf. The stamen recoils from his hand. He read a monograph recently purporting to prove that plants are sensate beings, responsive to pleasure and pain. It was a disappointment to him. He has been contemplating decapitating the lot.

The wooden sign hanging from the gallows bears the inscription, Sir Arthur Clarendon Mountbank. It is gloomy inside, a sallow light penetrates the canvas. Von Last has transcribed for his friend some of the finer pieces of Lewdwig Baitoffen and recorded them at the organ. The music is piped in now, softly, in *contrabasso*: it can be raised to muffle cries.

Mountbank shows them each a chair. "I think," he says, "the higher music of civilization blends well with the moans of the tortured, as though perhaps it found inspiration in them. It is one of the paradoxes of humanity."

He removes his gloves and puts them in his derby which he places on the table. His small eyes are almost concealed below a heavy epicanthic fold. Hans is perched upon a stool, his head cocked so that his monocled eye faces forward, enlarged like the eye of a bird of prey, hands still in his pockets, against his pacifiers, arms akimbo like a pair of half open wings.

"May I have a last smoke?" asks Slim.

"Be my guest," Sir Arthur says.

Slim sticks an index finger in his mouth, draws deeply, withdraws the finger, and sends a cloud of air upwards. He sighs.

"It's that time of day," says Tom. "I always tell him a story before he goes to sleep."

"You want also maybe the services of a priest and whore?" Hans scowls.

Both Tom and Slim have removed their hats and placed them on the table.

"Hans, please," Mountbank says, raising a hand. "Manners, manners. Let him tell his tale."

And so Tom speaks.

"Whilom," he says, "in Chicagotown, there lived a moll named Little Red Ripping Hook. She was attached to the House of Grandma, which was at the time also known as the Grandma Family.

"One day, Grandma was sick (which if you know the lingo means she was in need), so Mudder said to Little Red Ripping Hook, here's a lunch basket with some buns, dearie, and under the buns is a pound of horse (which is jive talk for heroin), now you take it direct to Grandma and don't tarry or try to cut the horse or make any deals with the Wolf.

"Now Little Red Ripping Hook did not need all these admonitions for she was among other things a runner in good standing and had had besides previous altercations with the leader of the other House whose Boss as you already know has been introduced as Wolf. He was given this nickname because his eye teeth were extra long and also because he had a long wet nose.

"Anyway, Little Red had that afternoon an appointment with a fellow in Sumatra, representative of a drug corporation, to consummate an ever bigger deal, so she decided to take a short cut through a dark wood, even though she knew it was part of the turf of the Wolf family. So off she went, her lunch basket held in the crook of the elbow of one arm, her hook brandished in the air before her and her three-dollar cigar clenched between her teeth."

He pauses.

"Ach!" says Hans, sitting on his hands and fidgeting, "der sushpench ist killink me! Go hon, go hon!"

Sir Arthur whips out a .44 magnum and points it at von Last. "Once more, Herr Furst — abuse the English once more — and I draw the curtain on your act."

The monocle has fallen from the eye of Hans, looking down the hollow end of the muzzle of the .44.

"After all these years," he says, "a .44— and here I thought you never carried more than a bare bodkin."

He shakes his head over the shame and duplicity of it.

"Can I finish the story?" Tom interrupts.

"Ach!" says Hans, "the story, Yes. Finish." It is a listless voice which he uses to say this, as though the heart had gone out of him.

"Meanwhile," Tom resumes, "Mudder used the red phone to call Wolf and tip him off that Little Red was on the way. The fix was on. Wolf and Mudder had plans to cut the horse between them. So naturally Wolf was there when Little Red came down the path whistling a tune from her favorite opera.

"Now it should be known that Wolf had absolutely no faith in Mudder, it being obvious that if she could finger Little Red, why not himself at some more propitious time? Furthermore, from the year of the flood he had yearned intensely to possess Little Red and dreamed that he might be, so to speak, the frog to her Fairy Princess.

"It was therefore to show his affection that he jumped and tried to rape her when she came by. She extinguished her cigar on his wet nose and laughed and went her way. He knew from that experience she was to be a difficult customer. It would be hard to snap her garter."

Hans is weeping. "Ach!" he moans, "my Gretchen! Ah say no more mein Lieber Raconteur!"

"Gretchen?" repeats Sir Arthur. The shadow of ignorance passes before him. He has gotten to his feet.

"My sister— my torment!"

"You? a sister bugger? My dear von Last, you astonish me."

At that moment, social history is altered by the natural history of *Bombus bombus*. The bee enters to check out the perfume on Furst von First, an essence of strawberry in subtle concoction with apple. The *Bombus* representative lands on his neck, von Last swats, the bee stings. The frantic Mountbank lends a yell as Hans jumps off the stool, clutching his neck; he trips over a mess of wires and falls against the electric chair.

Mountbank hurries to the medicine cabinet to prepare a hypo. They've been through this before. Within 10 minutes von Last will go into anaphylactic shock. The end is death.

"I guess we'll leave you now," Tom says. Slim points the Walther he whisked out of von Last's pocket when he fell.

"Wait! Don't go!" says Mountbank, wheeling, dropping the hypodermic needle he was about to screw into the syringe. All things go wrong together.

"We must," says Tom.

"I'd like to invite you to one of my nightmares sometimes," says Slim as he and Tom back out. He drops the Walther into the potted plant, which, if that is possible, recoils in fright.

They have regained the air. They cross a bog to avoid the open road, and then a field and up the side of a hill to the top. It is only then that they turn.

It is too far to tell whether the figure far below is Mountbank or von Last. He leads at any rate a column of mounted men preceded by bloodhounds with their noses to the ground; already they have crossed the bog. Fanning out into the fields on the right are other dogs and mounted men. Everybody is dressed in Pilgrim going to a turkey shoot. What Tom and Slim do not know is after Mountbank and von Last overcame the crisis of the bee, they flipped a coin as was their habit to see who would have the pleasure of the kill. The column on the right is led by Clarendon Mountbank, who lost the toss and had to settle for a foxhunt, hence the cry of tally-ho from that direction and the nasal sound of the horn of the hunt.

Tom and Slim squat on their haunches and study the situation.

"Clearly," says Slim, "the enemy has undertaken a double envelopment."

"Clearly."

"But look you yonder— I grasp their military incompetence by the throat. One does not undertake a double envelopment without a powerful center thrust to fix the enemy in place and thus deprive him of the freedom of maneuver."

Indeed, the road to the circus is open. The error of Sir Arthur and Furst von Last is, they did not think they were — in Tom and Slim — opposing an army.

These two have rejoined the road and head back for the circus. It is their plan, like in a thriller, to find Onedime, grab him by the throat, have him call off his hounds— and go from there. They are surprised. The air has changed. The folks have not left who the night before had been on the carousel and the whirligig. They had come to throw frog heads into empty jars, they filled the fun houses, the tunnels of love; they had let themselves believe the hawkers enough to lay down coin to see a couple of monkeys dance, or a 300 pound mama with three udders perform a striptease in a strawberry light. Who has not heard the cacophony? seen the spangle of light? the food, the giant softballs against wooden bottles, the belly dancer from Altoona doing her thing before a bear— the sound of coin jingling back and forth to thrill the heart of any hawker, huckster, hustler.

But now there is a different kind of pandemonium. They are tearing down the circus. Tom and Slim had been so busy with their own predicament it never even crossed their minds that the people here also had come to an edge. The tents are coming down, crashing in great puffs of wind. Cages shatter. Tom and Slim move like sleepwalkers through the streets. The crowd is bringing a nightmare to its knees. Figures gesture frantically, like waving at a storm, no, no, then vanish in a whirl of bodies. The two feel through the ground the shudder of spooked animals. The animal fair used to be over there, on the right, the genetic errors of monkeys with one eye and cobras with two legs and children with two heads. Tom remembers the cattle, up to their knees in shit, standing shoulder to shoulder in their feed lots, ready to die at the slightest disease, stuffed with hormones and antibiotics; the veal fed in darkness in narrow stalls, trying to commit suicide; and chickens that went crazy in the egg factory.

Here, to fulfill a wish of children — who always seem to surface in times of hope — adults by the hundreds rushed with them to the animal cages and lifted all the locks and opened all the gates. The animals — even the gouty, the arthritic, those whose teeth had fallen out, and those whose claws had been plucked, the lame, the partly mobile, the tormented — streamed out into a giant arc of wildebeast and zebra and gazelle and bok and antelope, elephants and lions and tigers and cheetahs and bears, leopards and baboons and monkeys and reptiles, wolves and deer and cougar and jaguar, the tapir, the warthog, the panda, they rammed and decimated the ranks of the foxhunters and then fell upon the Pilgrims hunting men (Mountbank died trying to hold his derby up out of the dirt. Furst von Last died on the horn of a water buffalo, his spine grossly shattered). Riderless horses joined the stream. The animals would go completely around the circus field before plunging south and dispersing, their roar and thunder like the cry of beings free again.

All the circus creatures have come out and joined the crowd. House trailers shudder when they turn over. Furniture is piled in heaps. Costumes appear everywhere, on arms, on the ground, in the air. Ferdinand, rushing, holding on to his knees, says as he passes, "They've gone insane." Tom and Slim watch him disappear like a great hairless ape beneath a collapsing wall of canvas.

Somebody has tipped over Warmonger's cart: he moves like a lump of jello on the ground, moaning.

No one remembers who put the torch to the administration tent. It burns with a slow and greasy flame. Tom and Slim had forgotten about Onedime when he appears. He stands on the edge of the fire. His skin seems to have been punctured in a dozen places and water pisses out of him in cute little arcs, like the cupids urinating in the fountains, until he looks to be no more than a loose bag of skin held upright on a stick. He opens his jacket then and reaches up under his chin and pulls a zipper down across his chest and belly and down his right leg. After that, steps out an octogenarian with a scowl, yellow skin taut on bone, a skeleton who had defied the law of gravity from inside a water case operated by an antigravity machine strapped inside the gut of the suit.

He glares at them.

"You win this round," Onedime says, as enigmatic as possible. He turns and walks toward the fire.

"Your ass," says Slim, "is sucking wind." The bag of bones Onedime sags, as though struck by mortal blow, before he can collect himself sufficiently to disappear into the flames.

They stand in silence, looking after him.

The crowd surges left and right. A man runs around dispensing free tickets to the circus. Others clear a space for a square dance. Tom and Slim join the celebration. There are those of course who see in crowds only the mob— the vigilantes, the lynch party, crystal nights, and people hid in shit pits while others seek them with flashlights; the sheriff with his trusty shotgun protecting the right of the accused to a proper hanging by the Law against an outraged citizenry inflamed by one or two outside agitators in the employ of the local business heavy who has an eye on the culprit's wife as a way to the culprit's land. Such mobs rage. There is madness in their eyes. They have death on the brain.

This is another crowd, a crowd of hugs and kisses and laughter, a crowd of victory (the fact that children have not gone into hiding is significant). Joy has been so long in exile it is a shock — a great exhilarating shock — to realize it is still alive. It fills the ugliest face with light and transforms it.

No doubt it could be said it's not enough to tear down a few tents and break a few cages. It could be said. And also it could be said it is not necessary to exaggerate a victory over a circus.

Around six o'clock Tom and Slim take their leave. There is yet three hours of light on the road.

PART THREE

The Passing of the Past

It was as a fantasy to occupy the time of walking that Slim reconstituted their journey. They had gone through a door somewhere, he said, around Washington. Later they had crossed a mountain, and even, according to one of the natives, were on a northerly and easterly course.

He assumed arbitrarily that they had been thrown west of the Appalachians, and crossing them again north and east would have brought them into Pennsylvania, so that now they would be either in the broken hills of eastern Pennsylvania or western New Jersey. So pursuing their course they would come successively to the Jersey flatlands, New York, the ocean—

Tom went along with the fancy, even though they could as easily have been thrown west of the Kitatinny Mountains; but he went along, even suggesting they could not have been thrown very far out of their time because the memory of automobiles is still strong here among the autochthones. He even remembered his grandfather, an old storyteller, whose favorite device was the dream— to either tell as a dream what was reality or ending a tale of the real as a glimpse into a dream. "Aren't there philosophers who like to think we are a dream in the head of emptiness?"

If there is a portal in time — a reverse portal where they could after all slip back into their own time — where could it be? For all they know it could be in Alabama or California. It could be in Latin America. It could be nowhere. They might never get back. They might have to wander here in utopia forever.

People back home would say, whatever happened to Tom and Slim? It would happen in a bar. Some would be sitting at a booth. The others would be at the counter. Everybody would have a beer, the draft kind, that tastes like cold piss.

The ones at the counter would swivel their stools around to face those in the booth. In the air would be the smell beer has when it becomes urine. Hey, I heard they were run over by a trolleycar in San Francisco. Shit, man, that's a hell of a way to go. Ya. ha. but it's just like them.

Just like them.

Somebody would remember they had been electricians and clowns. That would say a lot. One of the first questions asked of a new acquaintance is, what do you do for a living? A job bears an imprint, like a branding iron. Each was married once. The folks at the bar would summon the wives to memory, try to remember their names, Lucy bigtits— Sarah slabfoot—Bridget? Tom's wife had died; Slim's marriage didn't work out. Somebody would sidetrack their memories. Marriage doesn't work, they'd say. It rarely does. The family is going to pot. The old functions of women have been in flux ever since women have been becoming individuals, that is, persons with, for sale, an ability to work.

Slim's marriage (her name was Pamela, some called her Peg, he called her Pembroke) had lasted eleven years. It took a year to end, in one of those private hells where two people eat on each other's brains. It began a little while after they lost their jobs (he had been an electrician and she a secretary for a construction company that went bankrupt; the president ran off to Brazil with the funds). After awhile all that matters is to destroy or try to destroy the other before it destroys you.

He could remember none of the arguments— only the impression of her eyes that had turned to disgust and hate. For two years afterwards, from time to time, a simple statement would thrust itself on him— I know you, she had said. Sometimes it came nearly in a scream, with a finger punctuating; sometimes it came cold, over the shoulder, with a sneer; the first time was the worst: she had looked up and said it slowly, like rolling a turd out of her mouth. It ended. At last. Finally. Over. They were left quivering, exhausted.

Tom's marriage had ended two years earlier. It was another variation on the theme. It was in his ninth year of marriage. He was 28. His wife came home one day and said she had fallen crazy mad in love. He was, she said, the most marvelous of beings. He remembered for a long time the green of her eyes; her hair thin and smooth like silk. He had been rejected like a used penis, for a poet from Massapequa. He tried to hurt her: what can a man from the suburbs write about, he asked, used television programs? He regretted that. He regretted it for years. As though he'd scraped a blade across her eyes.

By the age of 28 a man loses the generosity of youth, he thought. By then the idea of surrender is too much associated with loss. He must preserve his personality, already beginning to ossify. Personality. Like a little bunch of black bags in a closet.

He quit his job (the same firm that later would go bankrupt). After six months a contact in the trade told him the circus needed an electrician. One night, a Saturday night it was at the closing, he played to an absent audience a little clown scene that basically consisted of bidding farewell to the lady who had shared nine years. He would wave his hand and turn and walk away and turn again and smile, exaggerated smile, and wave. Fulmigatio the Magnificent, a clown for 40 years, had watched him from the darkness and liked the talent and took him into the troupe.

It was the same Fulmigatio who took on Slim a little better than two years later, on another Saturday morning, when Slim had come to visit Tom and they were horsing around inside a tent full of clowns. Fulmigatio died. The management fired Tom and Slim for administrative reasons and, off the record, for their attitudes. The manager put it this way, he said, get the fuck out, I don't like your attitude.

They bummed around for a year. Tom was nearing 32. Slim was 30. It was to start again that they had gone to Washington...

Back in the bar someone would say, the last I heard they were heading for Washington, to get a job with a new circus down there.

Yeah? I thought they'd dropped out of the labor market. Which is next to saying, I thought they were a couple of guys without a future. And if the job they had is gone, the identity it gave them begins to fade.

The more they think about Tom and Slim the more the two become blurred, like standing on the back of a platform of a receding train. Who remembers having slept with them? or been told their dreams? or been privy to their humiliations? They never did anything noble— save a life or climb a mountain. Like everybody else they had just been milling around, trying to survive.

It would have been eleven in the morning in the bar, a terrible hour. Somebody would have dropped the first coin in the box of canned music. Down the bar three men would sit with their heads tilted back, staring into the flicker of the electronic tube. A soap opera would be on. The characters would twitch and rub up against the furniture and sometimes put their hands up to their foreheads, a test of fever that also functions as a test of sanity.

Marcia's husband would marry Harriet's mother after Jonathan's wife took Harold's older brother Ben to bed in order to punish Marcia for having been screwed by Honeypriggle's youngest son years ago under the stairwell in the boiler room, at the junior prom. There would be an uncle, peripheral to the scene, full of good advice. Ben's illegitimate son would sleep with Harold's sister who was the cousin of Jonathan's wife's second brother because she reminded him of his mother, whom he had never known.

And a psychiatrist would explain to them that people live in the shadow of their past, they cannot overcome it; indeed at times it seems they do not want to, as though all that mattered lay there, back there, somewhere, in the confusion of memory. Home is the place where all bad dreams begin. People are what is twisted in them. Enjoy it while you can. Try not to hurt anybody's feelings, and send Christmas cards every year. Don't forget to vote. In the end morality will prevail and the devil will get his.

The psychiatrist secretly flushes toilet paper down the drain then tries to catch it. His wife eats buttons, thinking thus to closet her vagina. The whole cast suffers from constipation. The priest thinks they are all anal-retentives, the sort of bedrock personality type of the age, but he blesses them anyway, for he is a sly dog and knows how to count his blessings before they hatch. One day all this turgidry will come flowing back to him and he will just have to sit back and collect souls.

"Tis good, my son, tis good. Go ye and do likewise unto the aborigines."

The past shudders suddenly then lies dead. The images vanish; Tom and Slim remember that world like a place they had visited and spent a bad weekend in. It had had over them for a long time the power of grief and humiliations. Now, like a twitch, it was gone.

The Tuning Fork

They have settled next to an oak for the night. It is a pin oak, six feet in diameter, straight as an arrow for twenty feet and then it bursts into foliage and rises another ninety feet. The Indians used to lay their hands against such trees in the belief that some of its visible strength and endurance would pass to them. Maybe it did.

Slim had settled down and leaned his head back and watched the sun crashing into the mountains in the west. Tom was looking inside his hat for two small loaves of rye.

It is then that Charlie Rowdybushes appeared and squatted on his haunches ten feet away. He is barely three feet tall, and completely bald. He makes a living renting space round these trees. He said he had heard that afternoon that a wave of laughter and glee was spreading east from the Onedime. He said old dust and must and all manner of dead things were shaking loose. He shook his head at the marvel of it. Tom offered to share their bread with him.

He rose then and came forward and squatted three feet away and asked them if they came from the Onedime area. Tom said they had passed that way. Charlie said he could see it. His eyes twinkled. He got up again and came closer and said, yes, he would accept to share their bread and they could have the tree for the night. He pulled at a fob in the pocket of his vest and looked into the face of a large gold disc that emerged. He said his grandfather, Adlebreth the Mischievous, had given him the timepiece and according to it he could stay an hour: would an hour be enough? because he chews bread very slowly?

And Slim said, removing a pint of water from his hat, he could chase the bread with water. Also they had collected a few berries that would end the meal nicely, after they ate the sausage, a hard salami actually, given to them by an old Italian whom they had passed earlier on the road. He had also given them half a bottle of homemade red, on the way to vinegar, but they could offer Charlie none of it for that had been drunk on the road already.

So Charlie rose and walked back to the place where they had first seen him and they saw he had a wheelbarrow there, standing before a bush, and he walked round the bush and disappeared for maybe all of five minutes. When he returned he walked carefully so as not to upset the wine in the cask in his arms. He said his home was about six bushes away but his wine cellar was just over there (gesturing toward the bush) and would they share this wine with him? It was a gentle red, clear like a pool lit from within by a reddish light. It proved to be a delight.

In ancient times a meal was not complete without some merriment at the end, Charlie said, for merriment is a most excellent aid to digestion. Like so many good things, it has passed out of favor with people who do not like to interrupt their worries for fear of missing something. This said, he produced a tuning fork, a bare four inches long and, holding it by the stem, he told them each to lay a finger on the stem; then he flicked the nail of the middle finger of his right hand against the fork to set it vibrating.

Immediately Charlie saw his grandfather Adlebreth laying the contents of a can of worms inside some Grand Dame's corset, while she waited behind the arras for him to leave so she could come out and be outraged. But Slim saw a faint glow on the eastern horizon, like the sky lit from below by the lights of a city. He asked Tom if he could see it. And Tom said, yes, he could.

They shut their eyes and opened them again: the glow remained. Slim said they had seen that glow once, with the night clear like this, from three or four thousand feet up, in a Cessna aircraft. They had been coming home from a benefit performance for old clowns in Binghamton. And the pilot said, yes that's the glow of one of the assholes of the universe— New York City.

Slim asked Charlie Rowdybushes if he could see it: and pointed to the glow and Charlie shook his head slowly and stopped the fork by pressing lightly against both bars the way he would to extinguish a candleflame. He asked if they had lived inside that glow?

Why — New York City — yes, Slim said.

He had not heard of it, Charlie said, although he heard Slim say it was an asshole of the universe.

Slim said there was no doubt of it.

Then why did they wish to go back there?

Slim said because it was home.

Then Charlie nodded, for he was wise to the ways of homes and had seen in his day people wax insane to live in places he did not see fit for dogs, even though it was well known he had no love for dogs and wished none of them well.

So he apologized for having been instrumental in bringing back to their minds a loneliness. He had meant only to bring them to a merriment. They had been such pleasant company, he said; and told them to take the fork with them and strike it now and then, think of the glow they wished to see and walk towards it. He could not promise anything. But it was possible that they could come to it. It had been done before. Not by himself of course. He had no desire to travel.

Tom protested when he saw that an edge of sadness had crept into the voice of Charlie Rowdybushes: they could not take from him this source of pleasure.

Charlie's eyes glowed at this. It had been long since anyone had shown any concern for him. Ah, he hoped they would understand he could not promise anything. He had to stress that. Still, it was his pleasure to help them find an end to their sadness if he could. As for the fork he was pleased that it would go off to collect other memories. When they had no further use for it, it would return to him. Or be returned to him. There was nothing permanent.

The next morning, he said the wine would spoil from the jostling on the road so he gave them instead an eau de vie, in a clear bottle, a substance of exalted aroma, he described it, which at root is essence of pear.

He waved at them, standing inside his wheelbarrow, so it would take longer for them to disappear.

Materializations

They walked for hours, for hours and hours, toward the sun, a hot alien thing concealed behind a mantle of clouds, heating up the air, making it sticky and wet.

Tom sensed an anger rising in him, a huge uncontrollable anger that sent spasms through his stomach and up the muscles of his back and along his arms. The sun, he thought, the sun was boiling his brain. They looked for water, a stream, a brook, a mud puddle, anything.

The television commercial had said, do you suffer from nervousness? irritability? inexplicable mood shifts? It may be the photochemical smog. It may be the electronic smog. And then men with smocks like pharmacists would come on, holding vials between thumb and index, saying, hydrocarbons anyone? microwaves? And a voice, in overlay, saying, do not let those little buggers get you down. Perk up. Take Mandalay. Take it now. Banish perception and sensation. Feel the world flake off. Then the camera would pan to shots of a thousand joggers in uniform smiling through exhaust fumes, while the voice says, this is your trip. Don't let em spoil it. The world can be made to look neat. And a blurb on the lower left hand corner of the screen reads, if pain persists consult your physician. Then cut to the main program and the character saying, What was I saying before this commercial interruption?

"We're dead," Tom says, stopping, panting. "We never got out of something..." He reaches vaguely as though to scoop up a handful of air, overwhelmed by a sense of futility and defeat. The sadness is all inside.

Slim shakes his head. "A dream," he says.

"Ah?" says Tom, "what are the rules in a dream?"

Slim guided his friend off the road and settled him under the dying branches of an elm. He held him by the shoulders and said nothing. A long while later he stood up and gazed on a land distorted by heat waves rising five and ten and fifteen feet above the ground. It was as though death had passed and left the land smoldering, the color of ashes and straw. He held a fist clenched inside the other hand. Tom, his head sunken on his chest but his eyes raised, senses it too. It was their world, their time, which was there and not there.

There was nothing recognizable in the scene. Not even the way the hills broke. But if they had come up to a door and felt a draft from the interior, a familiar odor of bodies and furniture, they would have known what lay within: it was like that. A recognition. Though there was no breath of air, no door. Only this land ahead, as though struck by death, the branches of trees reaching skyward, as though they wanted out, as though recoiling from a land full of terrors, haunted by madness.

Tom did not mention again that they were dead. They punctured their hats here and there to allow for air circulation, then they went back to the road. Three or four miles away, in a shriveled pasture, a headless white horse stood where presumably he had always stood. Neither mentioned it. They dropped their eyes to the road and concentrated on their march.

It would be difficult to face the world anew: not to learn it once again, piece by piece, but to be struck like an amnesiac by successive waves of recognition, anticipating none.

Spread below is a parade field full of marching soldiers in neat squares, like an 18th century camp, preparing for battle (in an icon of the same period the commander would stand in profile in the left foreground, proud and wooden). The white canvas tents are on the right. Beyond them are the latrines. At the opposite end soldiers are executing their third or fourth group of civilians huddled together to catch the bullets. The black powder, as always, makes little puffs of white smoke above the hammers of the muskets. Soldiers load and fire at will. It makes for an uneven staccato. The iron balls break flesh and bone. The earth receives the blood.

In the center a man without a hat (the general, for sure) paces, pensive as always. There could be a table there and a map on it. And field officers gathered round, waiting for the sign, any sign. Behind the man without a hat are pillories and stocks and flogging posts and soldiers busy at the work of punishment.

Slim takes Tom's arm, to lead him; and they descend.

The scene does not fade like a mirage would with the changing angle of sight. It seems rather to lose color and substance as the two near so that when they pass it is as though they bumped into shadows and the shadows turned and scowled at them for having been disturbed, and even fired their muskets and broke ranks. And the general watched them pass, moving his eyes only, so that it would not be possible later for anyone to say he had seen them, two men with punctured tophats, one leading the other by the arm, holding a bottle, their faces set and grim, with sweat on them big like drops of tears. A couple of junior officers drew their swords. Later they would be broken in rank and go insane and be led from the field and shot and their bodies thrown into the latrines.

There lies a field of tall grass as far as the eye can see, leaning eastward. On the left, which is to the north, monadnocks stretch to the horizon. If witches run around up there it would be time now for them to upset their cauldrons full of black and let the night descend from there.

Slim has taken the tuning fork from his pocket. Through its vibrations they see the glow again on the edge of the eastern sky. It may be brighter than it was yesterday. Why not? What fear of stumbling on a pack of stray dogs? At any rate they decide to walk by night. In an hour the stars will be out in force, the road will glisten. They know that dirt roads do not as a rule glisten, even if they do reflect more light than border grass or trees or shrubs. But they saw through the vibrations what Tom thought could be silicon crystals mixed with dirt, catching light. It was a pleasant thought to think the tuning fork was adding ingredients of another world to this one, because the other world would be theirs. They would be neither dead nor ghosts. They would be simply out of phase, out of synchronization, like any ordinary time traveler, in the middle of two times vibrating at different intensities. If there are dangers in this — to be caught forever in some netherworld, as good as dead — they ignore them.

"What the hell," Slim says, and laughs, a quick short laugh. He makes a fist and strikes a sharp body blow into the air.

Tom nods. "Right." And he makes a fist and lands one, saying, "socko! in the kisser!"

They shake hands over it and feel how much they are real. They laugh and of one mind they hug one another so to feel their own solidity. Hell how could they be ghosts? Impossible. They laugh and hear that take off on the air, and laugh again.

The frogs and insects may be startled. At any rate they fall silent, like a cautious audience. Frogs of course maintain their own annals. And this night is recorded as that of the Twin Laughters. The whole affair is passed off as one of those inexplicable jubilations which strikes humans from time to time for reasons not as yet discernible to frogs.

"You know what I want?" Slim asks. "I want to see people."

A flash of light bounces at them and when they move off the road to investigate they find a shallow brook playing in the moonlight, and across it a man sits on a tree stump, talking to himself. They look at each other before they cross the brook without really noticing they do not get their shoes wet. The man on the stump stops talking and peers in their direction and then around the scene, wondering what it is that casts a shadow like two men. His name is Sylvester Diary Hazyline. His friends call him the Gimp or Mary (his mother's name). The critics say he is, perhaps, *the* novelist of the age. He has a lot of hair, all of it gray, which gives him now in middle age the look of a man about town, sophisticated, suave, a natty dresser in ceremonial gray and silken ties, although tonight he wears a sweater against the possibility of a chill rising from the brook.

The shadows that had moved across the brook were absorbed by the shrubbery on his side. He does not know they have come up behind a cherry tree a few feet from his stump, and they stop when he speaks. "*The Softfall*, I think, yes, a good provisional title anyway. He — I'll call him Jacob Oliver Stoneloose — he steps out of the house, a Georgian thing, fifteen or twenty rooms, and into his car, a make of foreign opulence. That establishes him immediately as a man with no material problems, a man of the upper cut. And also — from the car — that he is a connoisseur of continental sophistication.

"His wife, meanwhile, is ringing little bells on the patio. She has an attack poodle, which suggests that in these troubled times one isn't even safe in the suburbs anymore. Her name is Alexandra. It evokes a city, a conquest, a lost world. It gives a sense of depth which is not there. She says she seeks desperately for identity, suspecting all the while that there is none. All the identities have been taken.

"Around eleven Hannibal (husband to Martha Lou, three houses down) will drop by to talk about his wife's mental condition. She will commiserate. That will lead to her first screw of the day. All in all the business will kill about an hour, just in time for her to begin getting ready for her luncheon appointment with Charles, the Stablemaster. Charles only goes with sheep, so she stays away from him. But she will order lamb chops and compliment the chef profusely. Then she will have a two hour session with the shrink, where she will evoke the love she bears a son she never had, Paul Beaufort Hazyline; Beaufort to evoke nobility, a dark knight, massacre of the heretics. Then on to a half hour in the meditation group, where she is learning to contemplate the essence of the world, a pin prick in a sheet of rag bond.

"Meanwhile Jacob Oliver (her husband) has called to leave a message he will be home late from the office. He wasn't surprised to find out that afternoon that Wilfred, first executive vice-president, takes off for the Minnesota Strip every night to see if he can't find somebody to whip his ass with a bag full of ice cubes for a C note. Live and let live, Oliver thinks. That's life in the suburbs. But Oliver, calm and composed on the outside, like a pickle in a silver dish, is vomiting on the inside. Life is tough. He has a peptic ulcer. At lunch he screws his secretary on the rug on the lavatory floor. Once, long ago, in his lost youth, when he had been up and daring, he had screwed the secretary of the president, Peter Alouishus Fastnickle."

Tom and Slim step out from behind the tree, intent on finding out who it is that Sylvester is serenading.

"Who are you?" Sylvester asks, coming to his feet, "a couple of ghosts from stories past?" They did not notice before that he holds a pipe in his right hand.

Slim looks behind the stump. He turns over a leaf. Tom scans the shoreline.

"What do you want?" Sylvester asks, following them with his eyes.

It is Tom who asks, "Who are you talking to?"

"No one. Myself. I'm running through the scenes of my new book. It's going to be my summum vita, the ultimate triumph of a long and creative life."

"500 pages?"

"More likely a thousand."

"Of decay?"

"Decay, yes: the kernel, the pith of being. Already I think it is bringing ghosts out of the woodwork. What do you think so far, from what you've heard?"

"It sounds about as interesting as a headache."

"Hold on!" Mary says, "hold on! No goddam ghost is going to talk to me like that. What are you? a dead heretic?"

Slim lands the side of his shoe against the buttocks of the Gimp, who wheels, pointing his pipe:

"Now you cut that out. I don't allow *anyone* to touch *my* ass."

Tom holds up one hand toward Slim and says to Sylvester, "Whatever happened to the morning?"

"Mourning?"

"The light?"

"Light? What the hell are you babbling about?"

"Whatever happened to the dream of humanity free from oppression..."

"Oh shit," Mary breaks in, "I deal in the real. You give me these inane abstractions. Convoluted crap. We're past that."

Life he had said once in a lecture (to students in a seminar on the novel), life is like a little black dot on your fingernail or your liver or pancreas and then it spreads until it is all over you and you're dead.

Tom peers into the face. The eyes are set, firm. His teeth are turning yellow, he is getting old. His gimpy leg feels arthritic. He also had a wife who fled. He said to her, before, I don't mind lies, it's the truth that hurts.

It may be after all that his world is real. And real these nightmares where people put themselves through the paces. It is a world where there is room for torture chambers and extermination camps. There is in fact no end to the ways to make men die. It is an obscure awareness of this (a word here and there, a news flash, like rumors drifting in from a distant planet), which is the undisclosed secret of their nightmares, as though, even here, life were an echo trying to return.

Tom steps back. There are those after all with whom conversation is impossible.

But Sylvester Mary has other thoughts.

"Come," he says, "come with me. I want to introduce you to a good friend of mine."

Why not?

"I never liked monkeys lecturing me," he says to them on the way.

"You must have been born in a silver cradle," Slim says. "I always had monkeys lecturing me."

"I was born on the front stoop," Sylvester says, "because my mother was too stupid to know her uterus wouldn't wait for her favorite television program to end."

Next he tells them about his father, who was an idea man in an ad agency. "You'd think that kind of life would be quick — not merciful but quick — but no, he lived to 79. He had about four cancers, three or four organs cut out of him. He mellowed a lot after they put a monkey heart in him."

What Sylvester Mary Hazyline has in mind is to introduce Tom and Slim to the mayor, because the mayor knows the police chief who, besides a dozen men under him, has his contacts in the underworld. And the chief owes the mayor a favor, who owes Sylvester one. Arrangements. Everything resides in arrangements. And these two creeps will be made to disappear into a bag, each with a bullet at the base of the brain.

But it didn't work out that way. When they got to the mayor's house (which Tom and Slim could not see), it was two in the morning and the mayor — who had, through the intervention of the moral's squad, sucked in a sixteen year old lass quite heavy of tit — was indeed rummaging around the mammary glands after promising her a full pardon for her indiscretion. The mayor was in no mood to chit chat with the celebrated novelist about two people (two men in punctured tophats no less) who the mayor could not even see, much less hear. And for awhile it was touch and go watching the novelist carry on a three-way conversation with one man and two shades. Obviously Sylvester was off the wall. He had taken his fantasies seriously. It was four o'clock or thereabouts when the men in white smocks arrived. By then little miss heavy tits had slipped down some sheets and absconded with a solid gold cross he had given his late wife to hang above their nuptial (and her death) bed. Surely the next day the mayor — who doubled as a judge — rankled to the marrow, would condemn some poor slob to death. Meanwhile Sylvester Mary went into the padded cell and climbed the walls. Inside a month the psychiatric assistants would have him eating out of the palms of their hands and wag his ass like a contented puppy when he came up to them. His hair fell out, his teeth rotted. After a year he would try to commit suicide by flushing himself down the tubes. He would be lowered into the pits, the units for those who would do violence to themselves.

Tom and Slim had been told the story of the child of six who was lobotomized for breaking dolls...

They walked until morning. As always the soft light precedes the full presence of the sun. Dawn. They remember an urban morning. There was an ugly warehouse full of old shoes, cardboard on the windows, shingles coming loose. Next to it was an old tree. Neither tore at the presence of the other. There was room for what is made and what is born and grows. There should be. A town is an enclave, a refuge. It is also a garden, an element in a symbiosis. And man, the most intelligent of creatures, who can also be the most gentle, knows this, knows it perhaps like he knows he has two feet.

Where there is grass the dew shimmers. There is a kind of electric odor in the air.

"Listen," Slim says, "before we saw Hazyline I said I wanted to see people. If all it takes is desire, now I want to see the world."

They have the impression that as they walk, the roads are becoming tarred and the walls of buildings stop dissolving. And yet even if they rub their eyes there are double images and objects that occupy the same space at the same time.

Desire is not enough. It is as though, visually, one time and its objects resisted another. By late afternoon they have come to stand on a street corner with buildings forming the horizon all around. Slim walks slowly over, stepping up onto the sidewalk, and stops a few inches from a building. The wall shimmers, undulates, as though it were heat rising. He passes his fingers through it and what he feels *is* heat. As though the temperature of what is not there were slightly higher, warming in the sun. He returns backwards to Tom. And then he notices that though he did not step off the sidewalk, neither did he trip.

"I think I know this place," Tom says.

Slim turns. Tom, with a puzzled frown, is looking up and down the street.

"I didn't want to tell you this," Slim says.

"What?"

Slim puts his hand into the pocket where he has kept the tuning fork. He pulls out his hand holding nothing.

"It's gone. Already, last night, I thought it was dissolving. Like everything else."

"Hell!" Tom cries, "that means we're here!"

Slim looks around and shakes his head. Here? Among buildings that cast no shadows, without a soul in sight?

Tom shakes his head. "I know the place. It's East Orange or Newark! Let's walk, let's walk!"

So they walk some more across the land of Jersey. Washington no doubt slept here on his way to Trenton. There would have been cows then. And wooden houses. The land changed. The rivers became cesspools. The fish fled. The oysters died. The factories came. Petroleum. Asbestos and electrical machinery. Machine tools and dies. Fabricated metals, primary metals.

Cancer came. There were still wooden houses, and women still came out of their back doors to shake out rugs. Where are those people now? A woman whose father, whose brothers, whose husband, whose son had died of cancer said, what can you do, why think about it, it's the price— I mean this is where we made our life—

The features of her face spoke of holding back so long they had become a mask of rigidity. She wore an apron, held a broom. The eyes had grown dull and mean. The mouth, thin and straight, folded the skin away on both sides. A spoon set the wrong way at the table made her rage. Any departure from routine was anathema. If there are vandals in the streets, shoot them. If there are sudden cries of anguish, smother them. At night sometimes she had the hiccups, like great tearing sounds of pain that would not identify themselves. She had found that cough syrup in little doses would finally put them down an hour or so before bedtime.

The urban agglomeration runs practically from Perth Amboy in the south through Newark and Jersey City to

Paterson in the north. Autonomous towns in name only, for they are like quarters of a city. Mahwah. Weehawken and Lodi. Montclair and Belleville. Hoboken. Here and there patches of grass. Some put flowers in boxes on windowsills, but the flowers resent it and they die. There are vacant lots everywhere, and rubble, and cracked streets and tilted sidewalks and endless little shops opening and going bankrupt. And the mob (Organized Crime, the Bureaucrats of the Underworld, the Black Hand, Our Thing, My Faith; also, hood, thug and Syndicate), it preys on them. Now and then the mob sticks a body up on a meat hook; another, chained to a radiator, is beaten with a lead pipe. A mob of friendly souls, with a code of love and silence. They deal they say in the unfulfilled pleasures of the little people, the common folk, the working stiff...

And there are the factories. And the ashen faces of people coming off the shift — Tom and Slim had seen those faces, they had worn them — black and gray lunch pails pressed against the body above the elbow, dispersing toward the isolation of their cars, to wait in traffic jams, toward the isolation of their homes and the sapping noises of television sets and the lurking trauma of destroyed sexuality, swilling in the processed garbage that bears the name of food and bubbly beer. They are not waiting to die, they are living.

Now and then a petrochemical processing plant blows its valves and a fine petroleum rain falls and people come out and curse the sky. The air has filled and never empties of the poisons of incinerated plastics, exotic elements, heavy metals, hydrocarbons, esoteric mixtures of these among themselves; the air, when it brushes against houses, corrodes them. The politicians speak of a standard of living, which is not the same as living; they say you never had it so good.

Finally, it is night. Jersey lies in darkness. But ahead, on the skyline, is the glow of the City across three rivers. It shimmers and throbs, like the reflection volcanic activity has against the sky.

Still there are no cars, no buses, no trucks. There are no people. They curl up, like a couple of bums, on a sidewalk which is not quite there, and sleep for a few hours. Later — tomorrow — the streets of East Orange will melt into the streets of Newark which will melt into the streets of Jersey City. They will be then on the shores of the Hudson River, looking toward the skyline that made Wall Street famous. New York City. And Tom and Slim could recall how it used to be that approaching it by air on a clear day, its own atmosphere could be seen, a dome rising 790 to 1000 feet. It had a greyish, grainy look. Everyday, upwards of 10 million people breathed it. The mayor said, I will not respond to a fistful of hollers, this city will not be badgered. You want to clean the air? Fine. These things take time. Progress wasn't built in a day. Meanwhile concerned citizens wished to have posted on all roads leading into the city a sign which said, The Air Is Hazardous to Your Health. Ridiculous, the mayor said. The cost of putting them up would be prohibitive.

They had awakened and gotten up and walked awhile when Tom jumped about three feet in the air and let out a yell.

"Look, look!" He showed the sleeve of his coat that had been against the ground. It had a kind of black and greasy deposit on it.

"The street is there!" he yells.

Slim rushes over to touch a building. He wants to think his hand only goes partially through it. There is some resistance there. And it is cool, like it would be in the early morning. And he can see clearly the mortar turning to powder between the bricks.

They throw their hats up in the air and jump and shout and hug each other. And Slim yells, is there anybody here?

And Tom yells, "Echo! You hear it? I heard your echo!"

They yell again, for anybody, but nobody comes. And yet it's there, they can almost smell it.

They walk like this all day, crossing Newark, until they get to the Pulaski Skyway. They follow its entry ramps. And then they stand alone on the wide road. The wind (they think) whistles past the girders. The road is there. It is real. They stamp their feet on it. Once upon a time it was the road to take to go from Newark airport to Manhattan (the heart of the city, which the Dutch purchased from the Indians for a dozen beads and two broken mirrors); the road passes over Jersey City, descends into the Holland Tunnel to pass beneath the Hudson and come out at Canal Street in Lower Manhattan.

On the Pulaski Skyway, at the point where the Hackensack River passes below, they stop. There is a clear view of Newark Bay.

"Imagine," says Tom, sweeping a hand to the south. "When I was a boy I retreated west with Washington, sucking the British in after us, so they could dine in comfort in Trenton while we spent the winter freezing our asses off in Valley Forge.

"Then I got this brilliant idea. I would fight the redcoats with weapons and tactics of another age. Read it in the history books. It's called the Long Commando Detachment. We slipped south of the British — down that way — through Elizabeth, Linden, Carteret. We boarded our barges — six of them — in the Arthur Kill, south of Newark Bay, and floated south, under the Duterbridge Crossing, round Tottenville and into the Ambrose Channel. Cold as a witch's tit. The sea wind whipped us. More than a dozen guys had old sheets wrapped round their feet. We hugged the Staten Island shore. The British had some 20-pounders dominating the sea lane under the Very Narrow Zano Bridge. But we never came more than four miles from them, by the sea route, they never figured us for that. We crossed the Bay by Swinburne Island and came in to set foot on Coney Island."

They are walking down the middle of the Skyway. Tom pauses and spreads his arms and takes a deep breath.

Coney Island...

He remembers coming to it once, from the land side. There was a little bridge with a sign, Trucks Don't Pass, Bridge Unsafe. And another sign — green and white —

saying to whomever: Welcome to Coney Island, the Playground of the World.

The bridge passed over a turgid mass of dead things, slimy and black. It was a creek once. The street beyond the bridge was cracked and heaved, lined with auto repair shops. The place was a collection of grease and oil, rusted engines, and men who looked like coal miners moving warily around vehicles, like hunters gauging how best to attack a dangerous prey. A couple of streets beyond lay Ferris wheel and roller coaster and parachute jump, penny arcades and hot dog stands and kiddie rides. Paint peeled, wrappers twisted about legs like dead leaves, dead leaves greasy and stained with ketchup and mustard; and hawkers selling junk for all the world like selling trinkets from some Egyptian tomb. In this world a hawker is born every day. Oh gee, dad, this is great (gree-ate)! And the father nods, and they laugh together in some secret knowledge of their pleasure.

Behind this playground lay the Boardwalk (that cold people seek to burn, summer and winter), and then the beach. In the summer a million and a half come to bake in their own din. In winter, only the dog owners and their dogs run; the wind sweeps across the Bay, mixing sand with dog shit for the next summer's millions to lie in.

Slim has walked to the edge of the Skyway and stands looking southeast.

"So," he says, "so you landed on Coney Island. Then what?"

"Well," says Tom, "we unloaded our six tanks, small ones, about 35 tons each, each armed with a modest 76-mm cannon. And then with the men riding the haunches we took off after the redcoats. The bastards were having a party in Crown Heights, with all the officers in white crotchhuggers, and the ladies in Pompadours, scratching their flees. One of my subalterns said, afterwards, shit man, you shoulda seen redcoats run, right over the water and up the gangplank and blowing against the sails like sons of bitches to get up enough wind to set sail. To aid their men, the officers on the bridges turned their fans to the sails and farted in unison. Meanwhile, George was cooling his heels in Valley Forge, suffering from diarrhea."

"Look," says Slim.

They have just passed the booths where tellers stood once, inhaling carbon monoxide, collecting so much per vehicle. Slim is pointing to the mouth of the Holland Tunnel. It is cool within. And with the light fading it grows dark. They had a friend, a beautiful woman, who never entered Manhattan by its tunnels: a passageway in mud beneath millions of tons of water felt too much a trap, a place suddenly filled with the deluvian roar of water, the sharp tumult, darkness, death.

The tiled walls are cool and dry. They strain to hear any but the sound of their own shoes. Even, several times, stopping each other and holding a finger across the lips and leaning slightly forward. Nothing. A drip in the drainage system. The thought passes through them for a moment that never again will they see a human face, hear a human voice. Only this, these endless roads forever. Then Slim remembers the tiles. They were cool and dry. And hard.

The Other World

They come out of the tunnel into Manhattan. It seems it is no longer summer because summers in the city are sultry, smelling of heated tar and dead rats and the odor of damp chalk from destroyed buildings, odor of decaying mortar and plaster. Now the wind moans like an autumn wind, pushing wrappers. And all the lights are on. The streets are spaces with incandescent lights. The traffic lights blink to the rhythm of their own clock. There are rectangular patterns of light against the sky where the tall stone giants wait. It's like — why not — a galaxy approached from the glacial night of deep space, with the certainty that life revolves around those myriad clusters of lights. Man made. Ingenious. Below the level of the street there is a universe of wires and rats, cockroaches, sewers, tunnels, ceaseless vibrations, bursting water mains. Above, vapor and odor and flying manhole covers. And lives, lives so dense they acquire an identity, denizens of the city.

But there is no one.

There is, a little way up the street, the curious phenomenon of a tree, surrounded by concrete. It is here, leaning against it, that Tom and Slim sit, and fall asleep.

It is a bell that awakens them, or a hundred bells. And chimes? It is the rumble of voices, somewhere in the streets ahead. And a voice that says:

"Good gaud, it's Tom! Tom! And Slim! Slim!"

It's Roland Swinburne, now as before, jovial, rotund. They call him Rollo.

"Where the hell have you guys been?"

"Utopia," says Tom.

"You've always been fuckin' mad," Rollo says and laughs out of sheer delight.

The two have scrambled to their feet and at first they hug him separately and then they hug him together and whisper sweet things in his ears, now as before: ugly as ever I see, same old swine, you took on weight, you lost your hair. They go a round of ring around the rosy, all three of them. Rollo quotes somebody's famous last words: don't shoot, it's me!

They walk north and east, toward Greenwich Village. The streets fill with people. Some carry chairs upside down on their heads. Others have musical instruments in their arms.

They had seen that once, in the aftermath of a riot. Television sets and chairs, lamps, tables, chests of drawers, clothes. Singly and in clusters, people had moved down the street holding objects they may have thought held the promise of pleasures. At least the possession of the objects showed one had a piece of the world, a share of it, one belonged.

There has been no riot here. Clusters of people stand everywhere, talking, a mixture of ages and races. The furniture carriers are getting ready for a jam session.

Rollo says to Tom and Slim they need a shave and breakfast.

They barely hear him, dazed as they are by the crowd. It grows more and more dense. It's as though after 200 years of evasive silence, everybody wanted to talk to everybody else, remember some old asininity and laugh over it, tell of some little victory over some little functionary, establish contact, laugh. Laugh. People who learn they do not like the same things gain confidence from that.

They learn it's not them, really not them, after all, who have their heads screwed on wrong. Sometimes (one says), you know, a body has doubts...

Of course there had been other signs (for those who believe in signs). There was the lieutenant of police who said he knew most police officers would like for everybody to wear a number tattooed on one arm. There were dead fish sloshing to and fro with the tide. And miles and miles of sewage sludge creeping toward land. And endless waiting lines of people with degenerative diseases, at the doors to all

134

the hospitals; and hot dog vendors with soda pop moving steadily up and down the line. There was the surgeon on a late night talk show who said of course the most permanent cure for a headache is decapitation. He brushed his eyebrow with his little finger while he said that.

For 90 hours or three days these crowds had been pouring soft drinks into the gutters until somebody swore, by the balls of a holy man, what if there are still fish living in the sea?

There is a joyful madness here, even the cripples feel it. Everybody wants joy, yes, the greatest intoxicant, the ultimate elixir. It makes alcohol taste like turnip juice.

"Did you know the Irish are celebrating in Queens?" Rollo asks, because he has begun to think they do not know.

A dozen voices jump into the conversation. The Arabs and Poles are celebrating in Brooklyn. The Hungarians are dancing with the Russians on Second Avenue. The Germans are whooping it up on the West Side like the Puerto Ricans on the East Side. Little Italy is going up in jubilation. And Chinatown is burning down eight thousand years of mandarin posters. The Jews are dancing in the streets. Harlem is in carnival.

A rumor had started, where, nobody knows. But are not rumors commensurate to the situation? Rollo and all those within earshot are not even sure it was a rumor. It said, in two weeks, all politicians with noses will be eaten, cooked or raw. And then the gangsters thought they would be hanged from lampposts if they were caught with two arms. Cops with two ears thought cops with one ear would be elected precinct captains.

A psychiatrist tried to calm them with the recent discovery that their diet was probably exacerbating their natural tendency to feelings of persecution, called paranoia. But everybody had cancelled their subscription to the word. They threw irate speeches at him and traffic tickets, and accused his nurse of not wearing clean underwear (a low blow that – good lord! — she was undergoing therapy); in a fit of depressive pique, held over from his previous convictions, he ran home and consumed twenty pounds of sugar and went mad, stark raving schizophrenic, complete with aural and visual hallucinations. It was then that he founded a new religion and ran off to the hills, taking half of his nurse's underwear with him as his banner.

Meanwhile the surgeons were having a field day; sometimes missing noses in their rush and lobotomizing poor suckers, but there was nevertheless a statistical average in their favor.

The Stock Market, having misunderstood the newspaper accounts about the nurse's underwear, was buying heavy in the expectation of a new bull market in bloomers.

The bankers, thinking Bloomers was a small town west of Bloomington Indiana where a new precious metal had surfaced — something called Noia — which was going to eclipse gold, the bankers were planning the coup of the millennia: they would dump all their gold into Bloomers and come up masters of the world. Even their astrologers confirmed this. The augurs were potent. All flags snapped from the top of the shaft. The moon was rounding, and Venus ascending.

"And the cars," Slim says, "whatever happened to the cars?"

Oh that. Funny thing. One night the gas pump crowd, the repair shops, the new and old car dealers, the manufacturers, their salesmen, pimps and assorted concubines, all had a dream. They had a dream and in this dream they were going to be forced to eat all vehicles on rubber wheels and all replacement parts for the same. The dream came in the shape of a memorandum carried by a high functionary from the State Department, one of the highest authorities. So they went to a wiseman, that he should unravel their dream, and spake to him, saying, what gives? A case, he said of the ptomaine. Oh god they thought aloud among themselves. The populace has had a surfeit. They shall maim our toes! Aieye! Aieye! Where we not good? Did we not see to our wares? Aieye! Aieye! What evil befalls us? Father forgive us, they cried, because we don't know what you're doing.

And so in the great hush-hush they stole all the cars and drove them off to Mexico and there they threw them into the sea, because they had heard tell that there the midpacific plate lurched beneath the North American plate and plunged, beneath Mexico, toward the center of the Earth. Surely (they said amongst themselves) if these tectonics are correct the populace shall never find the evidence.

Meanwhile the bankers had formed a caravan and headed west. They were never heard from again. The rumor is however that they found a pair of bloomers high in the Sierra Nevada and have founded a colony there to await the second coming.

The eternal triumvirate of politician, cop and gangster, together with their coterie of newspapermen and lawyers, were duly advised by a Justice of the High Court (who had himself received it in a dream, at the interpretation of which he was expert, having been all his life a weaver of the juridical filament), that they — politicians *et al* — had received the wrong instructions. He saw, he said, a great plain upon which, like cattle, the noseless and the one-eared and the one-armed and all their various and diverse entourage, were driven before a great wind that swept over them and covered them and when it passed they had vanished.

Quick, the politicians said, to noses!

The plastic surgeons, alas, were overworked. They stuck ears where noses once held sway, and noses where once ears knew their dominion. One poor fellow even emerged with a shod foot dangling from his forehead. Others came out equipped with two left arms, which gave them two left thumbs, a disgrace.

Rowboats were ordered. They lined the Hudson, from Battery Park up to where the Harlem River flows, then on to the East River and down to the Battery again, and round to the other, the Brooklyn side. Lord, nobody knew there were so many rowboats in the world.

Well, said the politicians, the cops, the gangsters, their lawyer friends, and a host of other spurious types — those with noses held them high, for politicians are a proud folk (oh sure with weaknesses, given to cantankerousness and murder now and then, partial to flattery, a taste for greasy palms, servile, inept) — well, said the politicians, if you don't like us, we'll go off and set up a colony of our own somewhere out there in the Atlantic. So there.

You'll want us back, they cried. Just wait. You'll come begging. You'll fall into crass anarchy, for sure, and creep toward cannibalism like the foul smelling rabble that you are. Mankind needs to be kept in line: without our whips you have no freedom. Have we not turned gray? gone bald for you? Suffered your incompetence? endured your fickleness? Go ahead, you lousy fools, banish motherhood, and patriotism and apple pie! You have cut off your own noses!

Generals and clergymen, who had gathered on the shores, wept at these words and thumped their chests and flung themselves into the waters, fleeing a sinking continent, begging for admission to the boats. And untold businessmen, who had gathered from the four corners of existence, in the hope no doubt of turning a sweet coin here, themselves fell into loud lamentations and tearing of the hair, then judging such demonstration sufficient, had themselves lowered into choice seats on these boats which after all they had arranged the rental of.

The lawyers were lowered into the water, as shark deflectors for the long journey. Gangster and cop set out the oars and heaved. The politicians, each one on a bow, faced the ocean and barked at it, make room, make room.

And thus, sad and motley, with no one to kill, they moved out into the Bay and went down to the sea. They took with them two of everything — two rats, two cockroaches, two pieces of wire, two motors — as it was in their intention to recreate the world in their image at a time more propitious to their undertaking.

It had been, naturally, overlapping voices that put the pieces of all these events together for Tom and Slim. And witnesses — mixing desire with perceptions — are notoriously inaccurate. It had seemed long ago, even before they left, that this civilization was like a huge dying beast in a china shop: no one dared approach it, each individual was condemned to stand aside and watch it destroy 300 years of labor and pain and promise. Now it was gone, destroyed — drowned perhaps — in waves of laughter. The freedom it had been trying to crush in its mouth torn away from it at the very last moment by a little chicken without teeth.

It was, anyway, a nice interpretation to put on it. And these faces attest to that, celebrating in the languages of the Earth. (Tom and Slim move south, into Little Italy and Chinatown, toward the old city, known as Lower Manhattan.)

What had they seen, in the other time? And if it were the future, who would come six months — a year — from now and put an end to all this exhilaration? There is, there has always been, from the point of view of the master, something obscene, something illegal, even evil, about a pleasure not of his dispensation.

Where to from here?

Already the tall stone buildings of the city may stand like monoliths: the stone idols of an age, already, barely comprehensible...

There are possibilities in time that never pan out. Freedoms — or enslavements — that never come. It is a piece of chicanery to say what has come to be was destined to be and is as it should be. In the middle of the 13th century the Mongols devastated the world from horseback. China fell. The Middle East fell, from Persia to the Sinai. Russia fell. Eastern Europe fell. All natural barriers were their allies, all armies standing against them mere victims for slaughter. They stood at the gates of Germany in the north and Italy in the south. And then a man died back on the Mongolian steppe: the unstoppable death machine stopped and packed its bags and retreated eastward. It would not come again.

Slim says shit, this has gone on long enough. There is hay to make and celebration to drink. They turn again toward the human masses dancing in the streets.

Behind them and below, against the solid stone of Battery Park, come from down the Bay and the open sea, the ocean laps.

New York, 1977